Alexx Bollen

ISBN: 1490367993
ISBN-13: 978-1490367996

# DEDICATION

For the girl in the black dress.

# CONTENTS

# ACKNOWLEDGMENTS

Thanks to all the patient and lovely people who helped me during the editing process. In no particular order: Tyler Howe, Shaun McGann, John C. Meyers, Tara Sager, Craig Bollen, Sandra Ling, Melanie Piekema, Colin Stryker, Matt Latorre, Andrew Drake.

Thanks to Stephanie Pendell for the cover design
Thanks to Melanie Piekema for the cover illustration

# 1. Tangents in the multiverse.

It exists as we exist:

a sidelong glance;

a subtle movement;

a suspicion of being watched;

the periphery.

It sits, silent, as the motions of the collective us move from frenetic to calm, and back again. It is perception, in the rawest form, made tangible by the characters playing roles invented for just that moment, only to be burned upon completion.

We see this through the useless eyes of the universe, forever in fear of observing itself.

The eyes of the universe allow for a story to unfold.

The eyes of the universe grant access to the periphery through their closing.

The eyes of the universe, glazed and unfocused, are looking away in wanton disregard for what will happen, for what is about happen again, staring without thought into the void, influencing only what no longer exists.

What is about to happen will unfold as it has previously:

A story will be told.

Characters will be written onto the universe.

A sequence of actions will be determined by chance, will, or fate.

We will watch them as they create a reality.

We will watch them as they destroy a reality.

We will watch them as they practice a sequence, simultaneously unknown and previously perfected.

## 2. Portents on squares of paper.

So he is called, by the forces of this unreliable universe, like the others who were called before him. His movements, scripted by that self-same force, to have him arrive at this point. This point, among an infinity of others, holds the proper arrangement of players and pieces to allow for a game, a story, to be played until completion.

They exist in a universe of perceptions over substance; in a universe of Quantum over Newtonian; in a universe where action causes effect without thoughts of distance or method.

They exist in a world where words can be made manifest, and the smallest movements in their periphery can hold the same weight as the obvious motions of life as perceived.

They exist, unbeknownst to them, in a world where thought and vision can be made manifest. They exist in a world of government checks and unskilled labor. They exist upon a tabletop newspaper, its white spaces slowly filling with pencil.

A man, John, and woman, Maggie, sit with newspapers splayed around them like decorations.

They, John and Maggie, abide in an apartment made from yellowing walls, chipped corners, and hope for better things to come. They chatter in hushed words and subtle jokes, reading, searching the want-ads with the patience of rent. They look on in silence as pencil-marks slowly fill the ink-empty spaces.

His search is dying, fruitless since the well of menial jobs had dried. His stacks have dwindled, his energy surcease. The sounds of a paused Nintendo game paint audio upon the scene.

She has been a help to him since the days of collegiate nightmares and drunken movie nights. In those days, before the joblessness, before the sweeping romance, before the calling which will soon occur, they spent hours chatting trivially about the events of film, the happenstances of art.

He is, and was, a proponent of the middle path. He sees, and saw, the world as the expression of something else, not the thing itself. In that expression of the world he finds that he cannot make decisions well, both sides often appearing as equal. Maggie, as the voice of reason, has the innate ability to press him towards those coin-flip decisions.

This is the world as it has been perceived; until today when an innocuous want-ad begins a set of changes, which will alter the face of reality, as ascertained.

They are currently browsing in a newspaper, the last place to look in a world of electric job finders and e-mail notifications. So it is that the page turns, and so it is that he begins to unravel what came before.

The ad is small, nondescript. The ad finds the man's eye quickly. The woman follows his finger as he reads aloud over the faint hints of the 8-bit orchestration from "The Legend of Zelda."

He reads:

> **Wanted: Someone in 20's. Artistic disposition. Poor work history a plus. Competitive pay, benefits after successful training period. Bring paper bag. No need to knock. - HJ Bonobus Corp.**

John's work history is not the most sterling thing; the last job he held for more than a month was stripping the paint from walls, followed by the adding of new. He is reticent to return to that repetitive life. With a head full of memories of chalky air and the smell of varnish, he finds the ad impossible to ignore. He finds the ad perfect. What he cannot find, however, is the company listed.

The Internet provides only vague references and dead ends. He is desperate for a lead out of his current predicament. They both dream of something better. They both hope that the path contains something aside from aging into a desk while wondering what could have been.

He once studied words and music at the local university. His creative push crumbling more and more as the months and years pass. The long days of fruitless jobs have stolen from him his lust for the creative, his longing for impact.

She, before arriving to this place, painted on the walls of her childhood and acted for no money in the hypothetical spaces between diners, bars, and other easy paychecks. They sat, studious and hopeful at the plain lettering and nondescript locality. They are intrigued.

"I don't get it. How can there be no reference to this place anywhere? How are we supposed to apply?"

"Maybe it's a joke, like one of those groups that all dress the same and run into malls." Maggie is smiling, leading him towards speaking in his professor voice.

"Those are called flash mobs. But this doesn't seem to fit. Those are all social media driven. I think this place is just old fashioned."

"Yes," she placates his answer, "that makes sense. It's been a long time since I knew about a company that can exist off the grid."

"It has been a few years. How did people find companies before the Internet?"

"Phone book?"

"Great idea! Where can I find a phone book? I ruined ours in an attempt to tear it in half."

"Wait, what? Why would you even consider trying that?"

“I saw a thing on TV. It's just a trick. No strength involved, supposedly. So, how, other than waiting for its arrival, does one find a phone book?”

“The library?”

“Sunday, closed after Three.”

“Cassiel probably has one. Or at the very least he will have an hour long explanation of how phone books are a government plot to spy on the elderly, and then go into his elaborate plans to expatriate.”

“Well done Mrs. Maggie, he does strike me as the phone book ownership type. Hopefully I won’t get trapped into another speech about the secret societies living on the fringe of town which intend on brainwashing us with secret government techniques.”

“Oh god, the dinner party at Eric’s! I thought he was going to kick us out when Cass went into the thing about reptiles from another dimension being the royal family.”

She, and this is unknown yet, is having a minuscule flash of memory or cognition at that moment, a yellow thing dusted on a shelf. She looks at John as he struggles into his shoes.

“Why don't you just untie them?”

“It's easier this way.” his face red with effort as the shoe finally slips on. “See, simpler than all that knot business. Care to join me?”

“I have things to get done, have fun. Good luck.”

“Thanks. I can't believe I have to walk to a sundries store to find a book just to find a business. It's so archaic.”

They embrace and lightly kiss. As he leaves, the apartment turns from blue to white, a shade for waiting and the doing of unimportant chores.

He walks, his red sneakers blurring in a half-skip-up-the-curbas-a-car-brushes-your-heel pace. John nods at the honking annoyance and continues his path towards the block of stores, which demarcate the beginning of the town center.

He has lived in this place's orbit for almost the entirety of the seven years since first arriving at college. His postgraduate work of playing video games and producing no great works has dominated his life since those auspicious days of three years previous. To the fanfare and glowing happiness of no one save for the disintegrating rags of his shrinking social circle, he spins his wheels across years.

And so he walks through familiar streets in the afternoon light, remembering and dreaming of the places he could be if only the impetus and the means strike him.

He sees a toy laying in the gutter, a tiny orange dinosaur next to a wet leaf. Smiling as he walks past, hoping to give that sight to someone else before it is swept away to the place where insignificant things like that are left to be forgotten.

The store at which he arrives is a place of ancient periodicals, sundries, candies, and dusty shelves full of bad records and cracked cassettes. Cassiel, a tall and lanky man with poorly sized glasses, greets John as the bell chimes his arrival.

“Mr. John! How goes it?”

“Not bad. How are things at the ol' five and dime?”

“Slow, as per usual. People don't care about useless objects nowadays. Thank god for your kind with the perception enough to see these objects' intrinsic value. Sad really.”

Cassiel is an old acquaintance of John's, a friendship formed over novel drinks and obscure records. Two years previous, Cassiel had found himself in ownership of a small curio shop half a block off the main drag. He has slowly turned that shop into an enclave of dusty ephemera suited to artists and hipsters. He makes his meager living off of John and the few other liked minded sort that linger on after College-Up-The-Road's season comes to a close.

"Yeah, well next I get a few dollars to spare I'll take those old educational 45s off your hands. Anyway, I have a favor to ask of you."

"Yeah, ask away."

"Do you have a phone book lying around anywhere? I need some info on this ad I found in the paper."

The man behind the counter's eyebrow rises quizzically. The man behind the counter has an inkling to John's inquiries.

"Why not just look it up on the computer?"

"Well, that's the thing. I can't find any reference to it. The company has literally zero Internet presence so, naturally, I am curious. Seems like an interesting place to work… I think."

"I'll give a look. I believe there is one around here anyway. So, you don't like the Internet?"

"No, the Internet is fine. However, in this day and age, to find out that a company can exist without reference to its existence anywhere on-line is intriguing to me."

"Ah! So happens you are in luck! I happen to have a phone book from about four years ago. It should be pretty up to date concerning a business unavailable to the Internet."

John thanks the bespectacled man and takes the large yellow book. Opening it to find an index, or a form of primal glossary, he sees in the opening pages a tiny, altered, advertisement. Unreadable through marker scribbles, the square, once an ad for another company, has scrawling handwriting across its face:

> *HJ Bonobus Corp. We bring ourselves and expect the same. Follow the dirt road until we appear. 23 Mill Way*

"No phone number… of course. Thanks Cass, much

appreciated."

"No problem… if he's still there, tell the fat man I said hello."

John looks at him puzzled.

"There aren't many companies that place phone book clues in advance of needing new employees. Good luck, check back in if you can."

"I will. You know the place? What kind of job is it?"

"It's not for me to say. Keep your eyes open and be honest. You will do fine in the interview." he says, walking towards a back room, waving over his shoulder.

"Thanks."

As John opens the door to leave, the bell chimes and he faintly hears a giggle from the shelves.

'Onward and upward,' he thinks, 'at least this place should prove interesting.'

On the walk back to Maggie he muses on the possibilities this place could offer. Would he be an administrator, an office drone, a secretary? His footsteps fall faster as he approaches closer to the vortex of home. Would he even get an interview? He nods to his extinct plastic friend as he walks past. No time for reunions, there is news to report.

## 3. Insect Life.

There are no pronouns, as of yet, but he is waiting, bristling in an as yet unknown corner.

If the universe could perceive without influence, it would watch him crawl and scratch in a dark and lonely place.

A time of changes is, yet again, set upon the town and the players held therein.

The pieces move in clockwork madness, inscribed in years gone by, and recited, by rote, as the night swallows the day.

There are no pronouns as of yet, and the camera of the universe needs servicing.

John walks from a small shop, half a block off the street, wiping his hands on his pants as he jogs the sagging steps leading up the side of a featureless two-story building.

# 4. Returns

"So, I just show up? I mean, I don't even know if this is a real business, or if I'm even qualified for the job."

"Well, what's there to lose? Worst case scenario you don't get the job and you waste a few hours, which you have more than enough to spare."

In an apartment above a long defunct Laundromat, John and Maggie discuss the events of the day. They sit on a disintegrating couch, held together by hope, and a patchwork of cloth remnants. John fidgets for a comfortable place as she sits stoic, waiting for elaboration.

"Yeah, I mean, it could be fun to get a job which I don't have any preparation for and run with it. What if it's some kind of serial killer's trap? The address puts it deep in the outskirts, those old logging-roads in the woods where the cults used to form."

The ideas of dead ends, horror films, and a maniacal plan to enslave him in a basement flash through his imagination.

Maggie, on the other hand, is founded in a more rational world. However, she is also fond of John, and lets him go off on his whims and flights of fancy.

"John… listen to yourself. Do you honestly believe that an organization would go through all that trouble just to kill a random job seeker?"

"Fair point, but stranger things have happened before. Remember Waco?"

"You've been spending too much time around that sundries shop. And, to further the point, if you went missing there would be a trail a mile long pointing at that place."

"So, you think I should go?"

"Do as thou wilt. That's all me and Aleister Crowley ever wanted of you."

Her arcane humor lifts his head from the conspiracy of maniacs in the woods.

"Thanks for the Thelemic blessings, but, I don't know. It can't be legal can it? It's too hush-hush to possibly be legit."

"If that's the case, don't take the job. No one is going to kill you for answering a want ad. If they wanted you dead, there are simpler ways. Christ, give me a few grand and you're dead, kid," smiling, she mimes slitting his throat with her thumb.

"Wow, that's nice of you. I'll go… I'll go. It can't be any more dangerous than here."

The next day John will prepare for the walk to the newly found HJ Bonobus Corporation. It exists two wooded miles from his apartment. He will wake, and walk. So John prepares for the interview, for the fat man, for the slowly growing feeling that the coming days will bring something unexpected.

## 5. An office in the woods.

John, walking down a desolate road in his poorly fitted gray suit, hat held next to the handle of an aged suitcase, looks like an antediluvian salesman. He leans slightly back as he walks to stare into the boughs of the overhanging trees.

John walks and sings wordless songs. He mutters simple nothings to himself and tries to remember the name of a certain philosopher from a certain class, taught by a long forgotten professor.

The office is centrally located in the middle of a wild forest three streets from pavement. Through the desolation of the walk, he ponders the approaching scene. Would he try to impress, or act humble? Would he be better suited as casual, pretending to know the work to be done, pretending to be the only man fit enough to do it? Alternatively, he thinks, as he approaches the address, would he be the only one with the temerity to apply?

He spots a mailbox. Its latch rusted open, flag melted into the dirt years before his arrival. Through the grime and rust John can make out the initials HJB, Co.

He has found it.

The grounds of the HJ Bonobus Corporation are a grassy field encircled by forest, a path of tan, arid soil bisecting. The house is of an older Victorian, purple, black, with random white trim, and bare wood banisters thrown throughout with little intent to satisfy architecture or physics. The house sits out of place, nearly incorporeal. It is as if a painting were hung from the aether, having gone unnoticed for long enough that it came to pass as reality.

There is no sign, or sign of entrance. There is no signal that business, of any kind, is done here. The dirt path splits, one side fading to grass, the other moving around the house. He is lead to the back of the dilapidated two-story Victorian on a dusty patch of earth, dead from infinite footfalls.

Sitting on the side of the path is the shell of a shapeless old thing. The thing, without definition, may have once been machine, may have once been plant. The viral grass springing from the earth is slowly swallowing its rusted/rooted visage. John's walk veers wide and right, crossing the visual boundary established by his frontal assault.

Beyond the corner, he sees a small child, no more than eleven. The child holds a clutch of balloons, letting go of one at a time; letting one at a time get caught in a large tree standing solitary, away from the mass of entangled others.

The boy looks to him with eyes half focused on something internal.

“Hello, I'm John. Is this the HJ Bonobus Corporation?”

The boy smirks and speaks in gravel, “This is in fact the property currently referred to by that name. Hephaestus will not be here for another few hours.”

“Oh, well, may I wait with you while we wait?” John is fond of children and likes to talk to them in such ways.

“Would you like to feed our friend?” The Child with a man's voice asks as he hands over a balloon and head-gestures to The Tree.

John looks confusedly at The Tree. From somewhere within him, a forgotten room of memory, he recalls the games he played as a child. He recalls a game: of jumping fences; of scaling trees; of avoiding parents. John knows this game, this ritual.

He walks to the base of The Tree. Its bark reminds him of scabs, the leaves of a black hole.

“Let it go?”

“Indeed. The wind and The Tree will decide its fate. Now let go."

He releases the balloon. Watching it float and seemingly disappear into the branches, he looks imploringly to The Child for explanation.

“Where did it go?”

“It goes as all things go, towards entropy. It is ingested and forgotten. You may know this over time; or not, so it will be.”

He thinks this strange child must be older than he appears. John think that he did not know anything of entropy at that age, as perceived.

“Sounds reasonable, may I sit?”

“Indeed.”

They both sit on the grass, in lotus position, and pick at random grass. The wait will be pleasant.

## 6. The Tour.

From the road the sound of a dying machine approaches, with coughing exhaust and random explosive blasts.

The child sits unaffected; the man turns to the demon growl.

The car exists more as chrome and rust, as smoke and noise, than something intended for movement or for use.

The car exists as statuary, honoring the days of the internal combustion engine.

The machine turns from the arid ruts and stalls to a stop upon the faint stirrings of grass.

From this statue a figure emerges, Hephaestus James Bonobus, a profoundly fat man dressed in anachronistic English professional attire. The obese Sherlock Holmes rises to his full height, looking just shy of seven feet. He speaks with a voice as booming and large as his carriage.

"Hello Child of the yard! Hello man sitting idly. I am Hephaestus James Bonobus. And I suppose you are the one who has been lately searching for my company. The Internet has been a-babble over this grand quest."

He wonders how this exaggeration of a man could have known that he was coming. "Yes, I saw your ad and wanted to find out what kind of work there was to be done."

"You see, young master, the computers of the world are the ears of the new society, like the Brahman, the telephone, and the mushroom before that. We use computers so they will notice us, like that pretty girl across the bar, or the loving arms of your mother.... I know...oh, here is the thing! And please, call me Hephaestus. Now, come along, we have much to do now that we know the way in. Child, I assume you will remain here, though the invitation is still open?"

"Yes. I will remain. It has been good to sit with you John. Until the next."

John waves over his shoulder as Hephaestus leads him by the arm. They approach a small cellar door, of the style used as a slide when you were yet innocent enough to forgo shame. The larger man and the smaller enter the slide. The stairway is dark. The smaller man follows the giant with a measure of trepidation. He has the sense that he faces no harm, but, for the life of him, cannot place from where this faith could possibly spring.

They walk through a square of light and into what can only be described as a reception area. It is larger than the furniture should dictate, gaps of hardwood marking distance between carpets and mismatched chairs.

Hephaestus waves his hand in a meaningless gesture, "John, let me show you the reception room."

A waifish young woman sitting at an absurdly large desk staffs the reception room. She, appearing no more than 25, is thin and attractive, with a pale face framing large, innocent, blue eyes. On her desk sits a brass lined computer monitor connected by random cabling to a typewriter with pink paper sticking up, half covered in text.

John thinks this looks more like a film than real life.

The woman squeals and hugs herself when they enter.

"Oh my friends! I am so glad and happy to see you again. The loneliness has had me staring sadly at this screen all day."

Waving her hand to the window behind her she says, "the things that shouldn't be there, but are, have been maddening as of late, all screaming and making a din."

With a slumping motion, she crosses her arms about herself and petulantly stares at Bonobus. In turn, he bounds faster than seems possible and grabs her face, looking into her eyes with a mix of whimsy and fury. She seems hypnotized, and then, like a mechanical doll fresh out of turns of the key, slumps down upon her absurdly large chair, behind her absurdly large desk.

"Oh, thank you! I needed that more than you could ever imagine…well, maybe not you, but someone else…who…" she trails off and looks at John. "Who is this handsome young thing?"

"Why Kali of the desk, this is John, a man of less than 30 years, with obligations to no party, save for his own self and lovely group of compatriots. We shall be showing him the compound this day…and, if all goes well, getting him a badge."

John tries to speak and is interrupted by a squeal of delight.

"Oh grandness! John we are so glad to have you! I'm Kali!"

"Hello," John pauses, overwhelmed by this onslaught of energy, "nice to meet you, Kali."

They stand quietly for a moment as if to settle into a new reality, a new set of principles. Hephaestus leads John by the shoulder with his hand.

"Come, I will show you around the campus of this, the HJ Bonobus Corporation."

The first stop on the tour, inexplicably to him, is the bathroom. In calligraphy, 'W.C' is written across a yellowing index card tacked to the top of the doorframe. The bathroom is a sprawling affair, covered floor to ceiling in once white tile. It is humid, greenhouse like in atmosphere. The tiles of the walls are creeping with vegetation, subtly pulsing in unnoticed breeze.

On the ground of this greenhouse is a half-inch of 'water', brown, thick with algae and shapeless plant life. John looks hesitantly at the great creature he follows, questioning what he is entering into.

"Shoes must be removed before entering this sacred spot. Please, no argument from the visitors… rules are made so they may fit the name."

John finds his throat filled with the lamentations and arguments of wet socks. However, seeing the massive man holding up one leg, without wobble, and removing, without effort, a shoe and sock, gives him the impression that this is a normal activity. It shows that the removal of shoes before the entrance to a bathroom will repeat a multitude of times, as repeated before. John leans heavily upon the empty doorframe removing his Converse and black socks.

He enters behind Hephaestus. The liquid floor appears viscous, gelatinous. He shakes his head at a vision of a fish in the water at his feet. He hopes, for the sake of the tiny fish, that it is a trick of light and not, in fact, an aquarium of the lowest and most disgusting variety.

Hephaestus notices John's look, nodding smugly. Finally, escaping his shoes, the water greets him warmly with the comforting memories of summer.

"Be wary. Be calm my boy. The world I describe can startle easily."

Bonobus walks to a sequence of urinals, stopping before the middle. He motions with his hand to have John join him. John, despite himself, does this and notices the bottom of the urinals have a kind of long grass growing in them. If he were more aware of botany, John would have seen Japanese reeds.

Hephaestus, noticing John's awareness, explains that this is a terrarium for grass and things to be explained later.

The smaller man begins to question the larger.

The smaller man is silenced by the larger man.

The smaller man's statement shrivels in the moisture-weighted air.

The larger man explains:

“Questions are for later. These are the rules. Let us show you the records room and get you an ID. You have the trial if you want it son.”

“What exactly…?”

A fat hand rises to the thin mouth.

“Later…your words will create greater realities towards the evening.”

# 7. The Hermitess.

The records room, as seen by John and Hephaestus through the textured glass window, looks like the nurse's office from any given elementary school, complete with the standard dull green canvas screens and matching gurney.

It is staffed by Dura, now sitting patiently at a square, metal desk designed with no thought of appearance. Dura, an elderly woman, slight in frame, with a ponytail of stark white hair looks up to the glass window in the door upon their arrival. She looks burdened by excess age, yet her movement from chair to door is fluid and effortless, the motions a woman more than half her perceived age. Her trembling, nearly transparent hand steadies to stone as she opens the door to Hephaestus and John, a subtle bow as flourish.

“Hello, John, my newest friend!” moving with alarming speed, she pulls on his arm, taking him bodily from the doorway. “We must get your picture on a card, in order for you to see the rest of the campus. Hephaestus, please leave us to our affairs. I will return him, in full or better, within the span of 45 minutes. Beyond that, we shall worry, will we?”

Hephaestus leaves the room, and with him leaves sound. The elderly woman and the young man stand, for half a beat too long, in complete silence. John shifts his weight from one foot to the other. She looks at him with cloudy, yet aware, eyes.

"Now, Mr. John, we shall introduce you to the kaleidoscopic eye in the brass machine. Be not afraid of the wonders held therein. You will come to no harm, as I am sure you heard me promise my lord and manager.”

The examination of the kaleidoscopic eye in the brass

machine consists of sitting in a leather-bound chair and facing the machine. The kaleidoscopic eye in the brass machine, as it is called, is in a variant form of reality an old accordion camera, gutted, and rebuilt for a modern purpose (if words like modern and purpose can be used here). It sits lined with purple velvet to be pulled over the head of the photographed, opposite of rational (if a word like rational can be used here).

John is slowly starting to get the gist of this place, taking it in stride that they would have an old style camera called 'the kaleidoscopic eye in the brass machine'.

"You must remain still for 20 seconds or face the consequences."

Her aged face like a rock standing vigil to a statement made, and made again long before his arrival. Her stance, motionless, reveals nothing of the ages which have passed before her once crystal blue eyes.

John nearly asks what those consequences would be, but thinks better of it, knowing the answer would be something incomprehensible. Questions, after all, come after the tour. He sees his face in the lens reflection, younger and much less glassed. He holds his expression as best he can, as the velvet hood begins to heat up. His look of approbation is held for 20 seconds, no more, no less.

She grabs his arm, and squeezes with preternatural strength.

"Here it is, your passport to the wonders of this horrible place. Walk carefully John the Younger. I have seen better men than yourself fall to the novelties held here. I have seen greater men than you invent more inventive worlds, more secretive doors to hide within, long before you came to bring life to this place."

Dura releases him with a sepia card saying, in an antiquated script: 'John the Younger.'

Upon the card, his hair and eye color are both listed incorrectly.

His picture, though flattering, lacks glasses.

He is, and always was, a wearer of glasses. This fact concerns him greatly, as does the dire ramblings of this ancient attic woman.

"Why am I…?"

A massive man bounds into the room, interrupting John, bellowing, "John the Younger will be released immediately! You shall poison his already fractured mind with your tales of worlds and doors yet to be known!"

Dura smiles knowingly at Hephaestus, "I have honored my agreement, he is yours, unharmed and unaware. Please leave me be until I am needed again. I shall sit and die slowly until then."

Hephaestus leads John out, whispering, "That was closer than I intended. I am sorry for any discomfort you felt."

John tries to respond but is shushed by the waving paw of the beast. He is lead through a side door, almost indistinguishable from the hall.

Inside, a foggy greenhouse, the mist forming vague shapes, Hephaestus holds John's hand. In a stage whisper he speaks.

"We must be quiet in here, for the residents are usually asleep and always hateful."

They approach cautiously, two doors, side by side, one belonging to the style of the house, the other of rusting metal.

"I insist, Mr. Younger, that you use the right, and I left, for fear we won't meet outside."

So it is that their destinations are weaved. Then, the yard becomes apparent.

"John, please let me introduce you to The Child in the yard. Boy in the yard, this is John, John, boy in the yard."

"I've already had the pleasure of his esteemed acquaintance. It is good to see you again, young Master."

Hephaestus plucks a balloon from the bunch nearest him and offers it with a gesture to John.

"Oh, I'm old hat at this. I enjoyed this game earlier."

Hephaestus looks surprised.

"He let you free a balloon?"

"Well, yes and no. He let me give a balloon to The Tree over there."

John starts to point towards the large elm, destroyer of balloons. Hephaestus lightly smacks away John's hand.

"Please do not point at The Tree. I'm sorry, office policy."

The child nods back and looks up to the small man.

"Please show up tomorrow at 10 am sharp to start this new, and I'm sure fulfilling, vocation."

"May I ask questions now?"

"Yes, you could always ask questions. But I wouldn't, and will not, answer them until tomorrow."

"Fair enough, I'll see you tomorrow at 10 am sharp."

"No. I will not be here for three days. Nevertheless, my faithful staff will accommodate you until the time of my return. Thank you, John the Younger. Thank you for the hope of continuing my important endeavor. And please refrain from giving away the intimate details you shall encounter to your lovely Maggie."

"How did you....?"

"Not until tomorrow, three days hence. Goodbye John the Younger, please do well. We have faith in you."

## 8. A brief interlude for dinner.

In the evening, John returns home.

In the evening, he tries to explain the nature of his new work.

In the evening, Maggie says things such as:

"You didn't ask…?" and "Who is he?"

John is patient in his answers, in explanation, saying things much to the effect of:

"I tried to, but he wouldn't let me"; "Hephaestus"; "Yes, I agree it's strange"; and finally "It's a long story. I could really use a beer."

Over dinner, in the evening, they talk.

Over dinner, John comments that his beer is stale.

After dinner by the TV, John shows his ID and explains his confusing glasses-less state. On the couch, by the TV, she asks why he took off his glasses. He comments that the TV is terrible tonight.

He repeats things. He again states that he did not remove his glasses, that there was an anomaly.

They quibble. They almost fight.

They nearly let the indiscreet moments of storytelling cause turmoil. Eventually, as their voices quiet, they let themselves metamorphose back into the jesting, joking pair of times previous.

In the evening, John pantomimes letting a balloon go into a tree.

Into the night, he pretends to be both a little boy at play and a large man grinning. In the dark, they are forgiven of the day.

## 9. Surprising doors.

It is now evident that the night has ended and it is again day, as the believers in predictive cycles foresaw. John is following a gravel path to an unknowable future. Unless, of course, predictions can be more believable, and less apt to fall to the whims of entropy and the eternal sense of wrong so pervasive these long years since the fall.

Walking down an old logging road to the office, the sun providing light company, he whistles on a dusty path. Maggie rolls languidly through his head as he paces an odd rhythm on the yellowing road, reflecting on his good fortune to find such odd people to call his coworkers. John, upon aforementioned reflection, is mystified by the speed at which his life can sometimes move. Years were spent in editing, waiting, every day the same routine. Then months of video games and want ads, the slowness of hours sacrificed in the pursuit of being idle. Now, walking to a job, one for which he has no training, no skill set for, he thinks, slightly whispering to himself, that this walk would be made better by purchasing some form of portable music when the paycheck arrives. John remembers from school that this area was called "The Burned-Over District." It was known, years before, as a place where cults formed. He cannot recall their nature, only that it had something to do with Pagan rites or the foundation of a new Christian sect.

Upon his arrival on the familiar dirt path leading around the familiar Victorian office, he notices the front door. He feels a familiar and growing disbelief that he could have missed such an obvious means of entry the day previous. Upon approach, he notices a rope hanging to the right of the newly discovered door. He pulls upon the rope thinking it an odd thing, not so much the rope, but his confidence in the rope as a method of bell sounding, that style of ringer long since replaced by its electric cousin.

Kali, the girl from behind the desk, answers the door wearing a dress of black silk and white trim, fit for prom or funeral.

“Hello, I am John, from yesterday.”

“May I see your picture please?” she asks in a mock professional tone.

He hands over his newly minted Hephaestus identification. She reads it carefully and jumps into him, giving an enthusiastic hug.

“Oh, John the Younger, you are most welcome here today!”

They enter a sitting parlor, velvet chairs and one giant couch with huge wooden arms on both sides. The arms are too high, he thinks.

“Say hello to the front room. We were shy yesterday and didn't show you.”

John gives a tentative arm raise of a wave, an almost inaudible 'hi'.

"You should be happy to know that the room welcomes you!" she squeaks. “Please stay away from the couch, that is for the manager and no one else. He has ways of knowing if it is disturbed in the slightest. Now, let us get you an employee manual and fresh cookies. You will find quite a bit of reading ahead of you.”

Sitting in the parlor room in a seat across from the couch, John is holding a thin, yellowed paper pamphlet no more than 20 pages, canvas bound. He opens the book, scans the first page followed by a floating middle paragraph. Having gathered enough information to guess satisfactorily the nature of the text inside, he begins with the cover and then in sequence, he reads.

Periodically looking at the couch, he thinks that someone had sat down while he read, that he was so deep in trying to decipher, someone joined him. Each time he looks, he proves his theory of company wrong, the empty room his proof. He pushes pack his hair in a primal gesture of thinking and dives into the mysterious pamphlet.

It reads:

*As you already have surmised we are a good people with important ideas, ideals and a family atmosphere becoming to a large outfit, which we are, as you will soon discover. Your objective in the coming weeks will be to learn the ins and outs of the office, and our satellite localities as well. Should you be honored with a permanent position in the main house, where you currently sit in leisure, you will be rewarded with a greater knowledge of our workings, eventually attaining the level of overseer, a position of great prestige. Soon you, John the Younger, may achieve this level, if our hunches prove filled with the verisimilitude that seems to portent most decisions of this quality.*

John looks confused at seeing his name in a book as old as this one appears.

It continues:

*Our policy is harmony through intelligence and proper awareness... safety is always a concern in this ever more dangerous world. Please obey all written and verbal commands to the best of your ability. Should your ability prove insufficient you will be, at the best, summarily terminated. Only through perception is glory found. The yard is yours, for any use. The boy shall not be bothered. Do not touch the balloons unless ordered otherwise, this is a primary company directive*

Pages flip. Words are briefly ascertained, time shifts.

> *Your job will be learning to observe the interior of the office, finding inventive, and time honored, ways of improving productivity and removing all non-essentials parts which do not contribute to the overall health of the company and the world at large.*

He tries to set the book down on the table at his right and encounters a sudden plate of cookies. He is sure they were not there when he first sat down. Shrugging, John places the book next to the instantaneous cookies, salutes the couch across from him, and takes a bite. The cookie does not know it, but John is changing brain chemicals in response to its sacrifice.

Kali enters the room, and the room fills with her. An awareness of the vagueness in his recent life occurs to him, a fairytale-like cloud hanging over his actions. He looks to Kali, a princess of sorts in Hephaestus' kingdom. The scene is set for something entirely ordinary. Something ordinary as far as the world of his office is concerned, which as discussed, is far from.

"I'm glad you're getting along so well, most applicants do not fare so well on this portion of the exam."

"Exam?"

John does not ask of 'the', being very aware of the word, and its varied and lovely usages.

"Yes, you passed with glorious colors and energy! We are pleased. If you could follow me to the yard a certain little boy would love to hold your hand for a moment and contemplate the meaning of what has transpired since you last breathed the air together."

Blessed be, they that live in the yard.

At that moment, in the yard, a little boy stands with his

balloons while a man watches in blissful confusion.

At that moment, in the yard, a woman with child's eyes watches over a man and a Child with saint-like grace.

At that moment a child smiles, mimicking on a deep and perverse level, the ways of something that more naturally takes his shape. The female is amused on levels unknown to John, at that moment.

"Oh, I miss seeing him like this!"

Kali hugs John from the side, The Child runs to the other. They hold his hand, smiling in ignorance and joy, respectively. The child hands a balloon and nods to The Tree. John releases the balloon and watches as it floats into the boughs. He winces as a glimpse of movement startles him from the branches. Searching upward, he finds nothing.

The child takes John's hand again saying, in a much sweeter voice than he had previously used, "Patience, you will see it soon. We have one last bit of business, with our friend The Tree."

The child walks John to the base of the massive thing, and plucks forth from the bark a small, round object, shining in the autumnal light.

"Is that a berry?"

"No. A branch bears berries. This is the representation of the soul, the permanent thing in this fleeting world. This is the fruit, awareness made manifest. Take this and eat it, for the flesh of the great tree is rare and only suitable for those of our flock."

The child motions to John to kneel next to him. John does so obligingly, out of an instinct the origins of which he cannot trace.

"Open your mouth please, and receive this gift. The awareness of the spirits of our forefathers is with you, from this moment forth."

John opens his mouth and the child places the sphere on John's tongue.

“Swallow it whole, and become as we.”

He chokes down the bitter sphere, his face puckering with the effort.

“It is done,” Kali and the child speak with one voice.

Listen.

Kali of the desk, the boy who is a man and John who is still learning, walk to the room with the too-large desk and Victorian computers which left John so befuddled earlier. She looks astonished as she turns her head to John, seeing The Child’s hand latched onto John’s.

“My! What fun! When was the last time you were inside?”

“Oh, I don't know. Time is rarely on speaking terms with me in these awful years. I would say that which takes my gifts was but half of itself back then.”

Kali's eyes roll up into a doing-math-in-my-head pose, “That must have been 30 years ago! You were missed!”

Kali hugs him with glee. The boy looks both uncomfortable, but ultimately relieved at the touch of his coworker, so distant these long years behind her too-large desk, so far from his Tree.

“30 years? That would make him, what, negative 18 at the time?”

John the Younger is still learning. John the Younger thinks in ways that worked in his previous reality, one that is still linear, less fractured.

Kali switches her tone to professorial, business-like, “Time is a funny thing sometimes. We will make sure Hephaestus tells you all about it when the time for telling is perfect. Now, it's about time to clock you out.”

Her job is important, she often thinks, and her attention to the details therein has led her this far. Kali thinks about work a little too often. She finds John amusing when she thinks about work and John's attendance there. Kali will think about John too often, and find him amusing when they share attendance there.

“But I just arrived, how long is the work day?”

“Oh, the standard eight hours, you will receive a better lunch tomorrow; I hope the cookies worked out this time,” Kali likes when John asks questions which she knows the answer but cannot let him understand quite yet. Kali is slowly becoming convinced John may work there permanently. Kali is becoming convinced that John is the one for which this place was created.

“Wait… what time is it?”

“As the crow flies, five *post meridiem*. No lunch so you leave early, it's a rule we abide by and adore."

“It can’t be five. I just got here.”

“Oh, time is a funny thing sometimes, especially when reading such engrossing material.”

She motions to the pamphlet on the desk. He takes it up.

"Please, study when you have time at home. You will see things better in the light of where you sleep, where you are John. this sounds off. Return as John the Younger at 9 *ante meridiem* tomorrow. Do not over indulge in alcohol. These are good phrases for you to hear. There are more tests tomorrow. But the child thinks you will do very, very well."

She tussles the youthful thing's hair and he shirks back with a face like murder. Kali smiles at him and whispers something only he can hear. He smiles back and they look to John.

He turns to leave, saying, "Well, I guess I will see you tomorrow morning."

In unison, they respond in a gleeful tone, “No, but maybe by the afternoon you may.”

She lifts up on toes and kisses John on the cheek. John mumbles a thank you and shuffles away, waving at the child. The slightest shadow appears over the boy, giving the appearance of something larger. Johns finds it par for the course of this day. He walks through the parlor, looks at the couch, and tells it goodbye.

As he closes the door, he hears a white-noise-like whisper:

“Thanks.”

It is time to stop thinking and get back home he thinks. This day, as abbreviated and as it seems, has done its damage.

# 10. Conspiracy Theory.

“This isn't good John. This place is not healthy for you.”

The growing incongruity between John and Maggie's view of the office in the woods and the work done therein, is exponentially widening. They stand with a messy table between them marking distance. The apartment sighs and groans with the tension of the lovers’ quarrel.

“It's fine. We are a group of people who have decided to concentrate on thinking differently, nothing to be concerned with. It's like a government think-tank, just without all the horrible killing machines,” he smiles wryly as he reaches across the cluttered table to place his hand on hers.

“I want to believe that, truly I do. But, you know better than me, that you have a history with this stuff. I just want to make sure you know where the fantasy ends and the real begins.”

“I know what's going on. I swear that reality is the same today as it was yesterday, and the day before. This is nothing like the thing after Tyler, this is controlled, fun. I'm here, alive and well. I know who I am. I'm good. I mean, this place is for real.”

“It sounds nice when you say it. But I filter it in my head and it sounds like you're training to go insane… again,” she speaks the ‘again’ with a lithe deftness, defusing the tension building.

“Hey, I never went insane. I just went to the same place as insane people,” he chortles. “I may not be able explain the things I'm starting to see at the moment, but I will eventually. It's really rather magical.”

John finds no solace in argument, no end game to be found.

Maggie finds no solace in the repeating and contradicting words thrown back and forth.

Maggie is disappointed in her furor but at a loss when confronted with other options.

She finds little solace in the humor offered as a cease argument.

“It says John the Younger in your book as well as your ID. So what? It's a coincidence; they named you John the Younger because that’s what the book has in it. Do you think that the novelty key chains at Disney were made only for you as well?"

"I hadn't thought about it like that. You have to admit it's strange though."

Her voice rises in a mix of anger and humor, in loving tones formed as cutting retort, "No, I do not have to admit that. I have to admit that you've acted like a rube since you first found the place.”

At this moment, a distant star did nothing spectacular; its light will reach earth shortly before the approaching asteroid, which will mark the last in a series of near-extinction events for the small blue orb.

She continues, “It's a religious sect posing as a business and you're buying it. Honestly, do you expect me to believe they have a magic camera that takes off your glasses… floating cookies…a couch that says hi? John, please, this is, I don't know, but it isn't like you…”

Her tone gets less severe as her speech gets longer. If John had counted he could have extrapolated that anger decreased at $1/3^{rd}$ argument length. John rarely counts.

“Well, it is like you. But it used to be that I could tell when you were off on a fantasy. Now, I don't know if you believe it or not. And if you do believe, is that belief based out of some sense of boredom, or anxiety; or maybe even out of a need to be accepted?"

Her logic does speak to him, her eyes, plaintive.

"I think I believe it. I think it comes from somewhere I didn't know existed. A void in me is now showing itself because it's no longer demanding to be filled."

"That sounds all well and good, finding something to make you whole. Nevertheless, I would simply ask you to look at it with some logic: A weird book of rules and a shadowy child with a handful of balloons. It's odd."

"But, it's that… it feels okay there. It does. They aren't a group of religious nuts… I think… I need to figure this thing out. Hell, maybe I can write a movie about it and make us rich. I always did well in creative writing. Of course I could be making us rich right now. I kind of forgot to ask what I get paid."

He smiles, and reaches across the table to her hand. She smirks back.

"Okay… John the Younger. You can have your fun but be careful. In addition, please refrain from more details about the secretary's outfit… I have enough worry without that coming into play."

"Deal. And if I fall into a Christian-Illuminati-Masonic conspiracy and they brainwash me into shaving my head and singing, I give you full permission to bust me out of that place, guns blazing."

"Blazing guns, check."

The neurochemicals of the room shift towards the darker spectrum. They sleep until sleep must end.

## 11. You've killed the birds haven't you?

It is the morning, diurnal: bed, and noise, and awake.

The two, who slept too late, too often, are now awake, and awake again.

He moves left. She moves right.

They collide in front of the bed.

They embrace and wish the other well.

He leaves with unexpectedly graceful movements in stocking feet.

She sits back in bed and tries not to think about his office, his work. Then, as the door is shut upon the night and its continuance, they are distinct.

He walks on implied paths.

John is moving, bipedal, to the office. He hums something indistinct as his gait settles into one approximating the end of a journey, ruminating on the office and the work to be done.

In a break in the trees above the street, a start to the sky, there is glowing in the aether. The sky is now a fading yellow as he watches the winged shapes perform delicate motions upon the horizon. He sees a singular bird amongst the flock and it seems more mammalian than avian. It seems impossible to have been given the art of flight.

In a patch of grass, a dog stands frozen, looking half-opaque, wavering in its consistency. It looks as if secret maths had been applied, as if a new geometry is forcing its altered shape and intangibility.

If, previous to this moment, John had thought about sepia skies, shapeless birds, and dogs of arguable transparency, he surely would have assumed he'd be terrified by their sudden onset. He does not have that leisurely moment to pause and reflect, to truly let himself become horrified.

So his pace increases, his eye line driven to the cement.

A bird falls to his right, bouncing slightly upon impact with the street.

He looks disturbed as a black shape bounces stiffly on the sidewalk.

Startled, he watches as another falls.

His nerves turn electric as yet another bird drops from the sky, and another, and another.

It rains birds.

John's brain fires chemicals rapidly. An instinct to run screaming to somewhere safe swells within his chest. To fight a murder of already deceased crows seems fruitless; to battle an army of indistinct dogs seems like a loss in waiting. He reaches down into the primal motions of ancestry, and runs.

He is now dancing, skipping; running terrified though the black mounds lying motionless upon the macadam. He feints left and ducks at random, a dance designed on the fly to expedite his escape from these flightless monsters, the imagined yelps and growls of animals increasing in volume with each step.

Followed by a trail of avian holocaust and wavering animals he rushes over the arid path to the office.

Breathing deeply, he runs into the office in the woods. His

face is wet with perspiration as he storms through the room with couch, and into Kali's office. His suit is remarkably unwrinkled as he comes to a full stop, and Kali looks at his pale face, glistening.

"You've killed the birds haven't you?"

John looks at her and sinks to the floor, holding his knees, "I… I don't… I guess"

In a moment of mercy, she interrupts his stammering, "Don't worry, they are only stunned. In fact, they are probably flying again by now. It has something to do with new seers of the periphery. It will pass. You learn quickly… John the Younger. Please, look at me the way you looked at the birds."

Although John has never been what would be described as an animal lover, he would have been guilt-ridden at the massacre of a flock of innocent crows.

Calmer now with the knowledge of his innocence, he asks in a sheepish tone, "So, they really aren't dead?"

"No, far from dead. Please look at me like I am one of your birds."

"Will you be hurt?"

"Ha, no I will not. Now please, this is important."

She is radiating from an unknown source. Her face begins to take on the aspects of the child in the yard's. John is reminded of the peace of mystics, the stillness of meditation. He sees her as a subtle gravity, a nuanced physics, concept over reality. John tries to shake off the hallucination.

"What the hell is wrong with me?"

"Nothing my dearest John, nothing is 'the hell' wrong with you. You are simply seeing the world for what it was, what it can be again. We're so proud of you."

Kali jumps to her feet and rushes John. As she leans forward for a quick embrace, her lips brush the side of his. He thinks that he has enough to think about and lets it pass as an accident of movement. In his near-kiss revelry, Hephaestus walks in through the door facing John. Bonobus smiles at the entwined pair.

"I hope upon hope that I am not interrupting anything important! Oh my-my! How my little workers have come to get along so well!"

She screams, “He killed the birds then saw my face!”

“Already? John the younger, you are a dream."

"Yes, a dream. I certainly have that quality lately."

"John, Kali of the desk, I would beg your company in the lower library. I think we have things to discuss now that young master John has started on his way into the mysteries of this place."

## 12. We're really quite dead at the moment... back in a jiff.

Once upon a time, there was a land of flying reptiles; of buildings hewn from fresh marble; of fantasy made tactile through the utterance of words; of fantasy made tactile through the slightest of glance.

In that world a man had a small notion at the base of his spine, at the sides of his vision.

In that world a man realized that there was no world.

He sat upon the ground, and felt the ground as sacred, and so it was.

He looked upon the trees and found them sacred, and so they were.

He looked upon the works of man and found them lacking, and so they were.

Once upon a time, reality was dictated by the visions of men, the idea of idea, the slightest of looks, and the precision of whims.

In that time a concept was formed, and formed again.

In that time, a concept created a reality that was unfit, that was too advanced for the people therein.

Once upon a time, fantasy and philosophy combined in the Eden-lands of youth to produce a horror. The energies of fantasy, philosophy, and whim, slammed together in one atomic push, shearing the world in twain; one atomic blast which made Eden self-aware, and forced the truth to the periphery.

## 13. I suppose we should have that talk we planned.

The library is a lavish affair in the northeastern corner of the basement level. It is red leather and gas lamps, deep cushioned seats and ancient oak. The library has the smallest hint of opium on the air. They enter as a group: Hephaestus as leader, dragging behind him Kali, and following is a skittish John, still anxious from bird comas and implied kisses. They sit in a triangle, Hephaestus the seat of the eye, Kali and John the base.

Hephaestus's voice is now soft, comforting, "John, I should very much like to know your thoughts on your adventure this morning."

"Honestly it's hard to take. If the past few weeks weren't so clear, so linearly stitched into the narrative of where we are now, I would say it is a dream, or a drug delusion."

John does feel, in fact, drugged. His suspicion is furthered by the ornate pipes and lighters placed as if by ritual on the tables and shelves of the room.

"Well, John, I could assure you that it was not a dream. However, as you so eloquently put it, the linear nature of your observations would make that assurance null, for I would be of your dream, and therefore untrustworthy. But, having assurance from my own linear awareness of not being your dream, I can tell you that what you have experienced this morning was very much real, and very much a part of what we do here at the HJ Bonobus Corporation."

"Well, that's little comfort in light of the fact that I've recently turned into sleeping gas for birds."

"John, you should know that when I was but young here the

same thing happened to me. It was hard to take, but I believe you will learn the control and insight to be useful in this important endeavor."

Kali, leaning across the hypotenuse of their improvised geometry, touches John's arm, her dress reveling some of the previously hidden. He places his hand over hers and looks to the beaming Hephaestus.

"Kali is a sight my young friend. Now, aside from your lingering doubt in regards to your awake or drugged state: How do you feel about today?"

"I need time to think. This is a rather strange way to start a new job. Maggie, my girlfriend, thinks there is something disreputable about this place. As you know sir, I feel at home… like I have always been here. I need time to think."

"And think on it you shall," Hephaestus' words melt in the air. He speaks with hypnotic fluidity. "Other eyes which have seen the birds fall did not take it so gracefully. In fact, if I remember correctly, and I do, your predecessor ran for his life upon seeing them fall. He shook for days. Though, that was before we figured anything about this out. That was back when we experimented daily with the periphery, with our perceptions. I found the dogs, if we may call them that, first. After that, the rain of birds was no real cause for concern. However, I ramble on too long about the old days. Kali, John, would you care to join me in an impromptu convocation?"

Her movements are slow, deliberate, drawing a harsh parallel to the giddiness of her voice.

"Of course, my darling!"

Kali looks imploringly into John's eyes; he looks back into an abyss; Hephaestus looks into them both. They are locked in a geometry of shared contact, shared perception. They are as if from one mind, one mode of vision layered into three angles, broken from a line and grafted through eye contact and the faltering minds of a man moving from past to future.

Then, suddenly as it began, the convocation ends. They shake off a collective hypnagogia and the room comes back into focus. John and Hephaestus take one last moment to share eyes. John sees himself looking back; he sees the microscopic fissures in the narrative of Hephaestus and the work that was done, and will be done again.

"Grand," Hephaestus turns back from subtle to ringmaster, "now let us make our way to the yard. I believe we will spend much time today in communion with The Tree, the child, and the ancient in the attic. Let us return here, when once again leisure is demanded."

John, turning to follow Hephaestus, sees a previously unnoticed door between the shelves. Befuddled he walks to the newly minted door. He has a vague recollection of a door like this one in a half-forgotten basement only existent in the shadowy memories of childhood.

The large man and the tiny girl walk through into streaming daylight. The smaller man follows with trepidation. The smaller man finds himself in a yard, facing a tree with a strangely animal aspect. The architecture of his exit seems both impossible and unavoidable, given the location.

## 14. Worriedly pacing.

In a fairer universe, one slightly to the left of this one, Maggie would find herself happy and content with the state of her relationship.

In a fairer universe, she would have found a man to love who is stable of mind, lithe of body, and full of prospects for the future.

In a fairer universe, there would be dinner parties and subtle hints to friends about possible children/marriage/housing.

In a fairer universe, John would be home looking for a new job.

In a fairer universe, John would find a job without trees and demons, without birds, and without ladies in pretty dresses.

However, that universe is telling that story, unbeknownst to us; as our universe is telling this story, unbeknownst to the characters moving within it.

Maggie walks under the boughs of suburban trees, subconsciously avoiding stepping on cracks, a preventative measure for her mother. She is moving towards a job which provides the means for rent and the provisions of life, no more.

She is moving towards her job where she may duck her head and dodge the responsibility of caring.

Maggie thinks of John as she passes the ice cream shop, remembering their last summer, sharing sherbet with no thought to the universe outside of themselves. Now, she thinks of him with great anxiety. She remembers John finally telling her about the pain that occurred to him in his distant past. She recalls the fright in his face as he spoke in detail about a lost child and the later invention of a world where no children would go lost. She thinks of her elated John, many years since his trouble, falling madly for her, and her for him. She thinks of John as a momentary flash of orange catches an insignificant part of her attention.

Maggie paces her steps and her breathing in a rhythm designed to soothe souls and forgo worries. Maggie sticks her hands into her coat pocket and looks up at the changing leaves.

'The world will cycle,' she thinks, 'I suppose it's up to me to follow suit. Let John be John. Let his world cycle and I will simply hope I can hold his hand through the process.'

On a one lane street in a nondescript town, a petite woman with mousy hair and an awkwardly paced walk enters a glass door adorned with concert promotions. In a purposeless shop, she masks her face in a shroud of polite banter with faceless clients. In a moment she is changed from casual to faux-professional, from Maggie of wild youth and limitless potential to Ms. Dee, of register one.

# 15. Staff meeting.

They stand in front of The Tree: Dura of the Attic, The Child, Kali, and the giant. They turn to face John the Younger.

"John the Younger, welcome to your first staff meeting!"

John nods in an implied bow, "Thank you for the warm reception."

"It is good to see you again, Master John." Dura, looking markedly older than at John's introduction, still speaks with force. "The higher reaches have been lonely since your visit."

"Hello Dura, it is good to see you again. The picture you took treated my face well."

"You are kind. Hephaestus, my love, may I sit upon your grass? My old bones have been wearied from the descent."

"Of course Miss Dura, your health is of the top importance at our esteemed locality."

The ancient woman struggles to sit upon the grass, her arms and legs shaking from the effort. The Child offers his hand for support. Together they sit.

For the moment of a camera flash(if only there were a camera) Kali, Child, Dura, Hephaestus, and newly minted John, sit stationary like a poorly lit watercolor against the blended paint of The Tree. The Tree sits as focus of this artificial painting that is life at the offices of the HJ Bonobus Corp. It stands as an idol in the eye-line of the staff, a golden calf in the shape of a tree.

"Now, to business!"

He raises his hands above his head, screaming comically. The group feels a pressure abate.

"As some of us know, John here has taken a significant step towards joining this office in perpetuity. Today, not but two hours ago, he killed the birds."

He claps John on the back and The Child and Dura inhale in surprise.

"I know, I know, the alacrity of this momentous feat has not missed even these old eyes. Today we spend time in great happiness for John the Younger. Therefore, for the rest of the day, I would like John and The Child to work together in silent meditation. I feel that some time with such like minds may go a long way to soothe the rift caused by this morning's pulsations. Kali please escort Dura back upstairs and join her in whatever activities she would enjoy. As for I, the world is broad, and the time is short. I shall be out for the remainder. Good blessings on you all."

Waving away the floating remnants of his speech, he turns and walks to the dilapidated car still sitting as if dead on the side of an arid path. The Child looks to John's hand as the elder is helped to standing by the young. The workday begins in earnest.

## 16. The warping of space-time.

He thinks it a cold thing, this sitting alone at a table, the light from the refrigerator having gone dark along with the hopes of satiety. John sits and fingers the chipping paint of his second-hand table. He stirs at cold tea, the spirals of milk making odd faces, producing a dream from a place of warm summers and the innocence of youth. He thinks of Maggie and her trip home. He is jarred from this dream by the creak of a door. From his dream, Maggie arrives in the apartment. He hears her breathing heavy from the climb.

They exchange small greetings as the food is moved from bag to shelf, from shelf to heat, from heat to mouth. They avoid talk of the office until the needs of the belly are sated.

Maggie is not in the slightest bit at ease. Those weighted sighs, shifts, and throat clearings are signs, as John well knows, of forthcoming battle.

"So, how was work?" she begins with a tone of conversational interest, a mask for inner turmoil.

"It was odd, again, odd. I think I might be having flashbacks."

"Your brother?"

"No. No. Nothing like that. I mean acid, that sort of flashback. It's just, to put it bluntly, this morning I killed birds."

Maggie is, instantaneously, confused and disturbed by his statement. Taken in context, she worries of serial killings and an excess of JD Salinger books.

“You what?"

His eyes speak of worry.

"When I walked to work today, something happened with the birds. I was looking at this dog and it turned transparent. I shook it off, figured it was a trick of the light. Then they fell. It was like rain. It was raining birds on me."

"It rained birds? How exactly does it rain birds? Define 'rain' for me dear."

He exhales into words, a fade in from the reaches, "Well, I was walking to work, down by the old logging roads. I was looking over at this dog and it was standing there, more like a statue than a real animal. It looked half-opaque, wavering in consistency. I was afraid. So I started to walk faster, and for some reason my eye line was drawn to the cement. Then it happened. A bird fell to my right, bouncing off the sidewalk. I was obviously disturbed. Then another bounced stiffly on the grass."

He pauses, and she looks scared.

Continuing, he says, "Then… it rained birds. So I ran. I was dancing, skipping, running terrified though them lying dead on the ground. I feinted left, and ducked at random, just moving like a lunatic to avoid being hit. So I ran to the office. Then Kali told me that it happens to people that work there all the time. So, I calmed down a bit and tried to practice in my head how I could tell you about it.”

"Oh god John, maybe you should get some sleep. Are you sure it was real? Maybe you did have a flashback," she struggles for a foothold in the maelstrom of John's recent insanities.

"I'm sure it was real. I've hallucinated before, but it was nothing like this. This was real. I could have touched them if I felt like that would prove anything.”

"Let's take a second to pretend that you were correct, and actually saw something. We would have heard about it. There is no way a localized bird die-off via half-visible dog attack would go unreported, no matter how far into the woods it was. It's probably stress plus imagination, plus the falling leaves. You're not used to being up so early; you imagined it. This will be fine… I know you will be okay."

In Maggie there is a picture of straitjackets and losing her love.

"Christ, I suppose that could be true. But the secretary knew what I was talking about. And so did Bonobus… the fat man."

"John. There is something very wrong about that place. You're in over your head. You can find another job."

"Not likely another job, but you're right about that place. It's not negative though. It's off somehow, like it's halfway next-door to a real office, with real people and real work. All I did was enter the wrong door, and no one noticed, myself included."

"What?"

"When I'm there, it's like another universe, nearly identical, but not. Like it's sitting half a shade over, you'd never notice it unless you got lucky, or looked softly enough."

"Maybe we should just go to bed and ignore the whole thing till the morning. It could be that they are no more than an odd group, no malevolence at all. They could be pampering someone who they see good things in. You do have a wonderful lump of brain in that rock up there."

Lovingly she lightly raps his skull.

"You're right. Occam's razor, the simplest solutions, etc…Bed sounds like just about the best idea ever right now."

## 17. A disproportionate amount of plastic dinosaurs.

Kali's voice is of whimsy, anticipating joys in place of information.

“No, John the Younger, I do not believe that I've seen or heard of plastic dinosaurs having any relation to what we do.”

“Strange, I seem to stumble upon a disproportionate amount of plastic dinosaurs lately. I saw this little guy sitting in a gutter outside of Cassiel's Sundries and it just stuck out; it was almost shining in the leaves. I thought maybe it was a sign, or symptom, or something.”

“No, no my dearest John, dinosaurs and the periphery have very little in common with each other. I have not had the pleasure of that shop's commerce. Next I walk the ways of the town I shall visit it, and maybe your plastic friend.”

"Must have had a sale."

"Sometimes a cigar is a cigar and a small plastic dinosaur lying in the grass is simply a small plastic dinosaur lying in the grass.”

Listen.

There are vibrations in the fields of the peripheral vision. Those vibrations produce some odd and seemingly pointless side effects. One of which is a rather strange predilection to coincidence. This manifests as glittering things in the grass taking the shape of dull objects in the office; moments of similar words from dissimilar places; and in this case, small plastic dinosaurs.

John vibrates differently in the situations where it is warranted to do so. The people from his past are revealed as cogs in the complexity of this machine. The relationships, forged before his birth, circle back upon him as pictures on yellowing walls peel and fade into nothingness.

Now, he sits mercy seat to The Tree and reads from the book of phrases from a once great man. Filled with a form of death too common to the passengers of the other sight he falls to the entropic pull of mystical thinking, daydreaming portends.

Hephaestus' voice rattles windows and jump-starts normally calm hearts, "What do we speak of now, my children of the lesser gods? Dinosaurs are chasing our dear John?"

John and Kali spasm at his bellow.

"Yes, John the Younger has had run-ins with dinosaurs, of the plastic variety."

"Plastic you say? Much easier to deal with than the flesh and blood variety, I suppose. John, we should talk about this in detail. Please, follow me to the drawing room."

"We have a drawing room?" John says.

"The drawing room is one of the most important spaces in the hallowed building. John my boy let us go there and speak of false reptiles."

"Sure, but it's just a coincidence. I'm curious mostly."

"I know my boy, but that coincidental perception does point to something much larger. When one is entwined with the peripheral awareness, coincidences tend to follow. Where we find coincidence, we sees signs of the periphery. Now, please, follow me."

The drawing room is a hidden antechamber to the living room. It has two chairs, bare walls and a small cabinet for bottles of rare liquor and unlabeled bottles of wine. The room, as it sits, shows no purpose save for a conversation between two, and only two people.

"John, we arrive at a crossroads," he pantomimes the sign of cross upon his chest, "the past and the future entwined. You are starting to notice the existence of the other things, even invented ones like small dinosaurs. This is a good sign. But, there are concerns."

"Concerns?"

"John, your growth of awareness is directly related to your speedy path into and around the awareness of the other place. Your, let's say, unique situation, could turn South if not thought out fully before walking further down unknown paths."

John's tone is aggravated, graveled and losing focus. He grows tired of confusion, "What makes me so unique? Is it that I learned quickly? That I bothered to respond to the advertisement? That I am patient enough to deal with falling birds? That I can inexplicably accept the story of invisible forces trying to destroy our barely visible ones? Is it that The Child lets me feed The Tree? What?"

"In a word, yes... You are special for all those things, and many more. However, what I was referring to is your perception of the past, and its influence on your perception of the future. That future being today. You invented a life to cover up for the transgressions of your past. We all do this. Now, your awareness is such, unlike the rest of us, that you may pull down those veils and see your world in the stark light of truth and reason...this would prove horrific, maddening. You are unique in that you can take yourself apart far more quickly than most others. But, that speed of deconstruction comes with the cost of possibly not being able to gather back together your constituent parts. "

John speaks with a voice suited to prophecy and the giving of last rites, "And that's unique? That sounds like being human. We are all one revelation away from having the ultimate existential panic. We are all one tiny truth from screaming madly at the sky and walking home mumbling about trees. Hephaestus, I'm not unique; I'm awake."

"My boy, you are correct. You may be better equipped to handle this than I previously thought. Remember though, not all coincidences are revelation, and not all revelation will lead you to better places. Let us not forget the lessons of the past, as we slowly write new meanings. Be careful John the Younger, or the world will quit making sense. Be careful or all of this will become a tool of destruction. Remember the lessons of the hill."

"I'm not sure what lessons you'd have me remember. But I will be careful."

"You will be sure of these lessons, eventually. Now, let us take to the yard, I long to see The Tree."

As the room ceases to be occupied, the door swings shut, and a bolt is heard echoing. As they approach Kali's desk, John turns his head in the direction they have walked. He thinks it normal that the wall is unmarred by a doorway. The house shifts back to one permutation as John moves forward to yet another.

## 18. Strolling Heisenbergs.

It has been wished, and wished again, for there to be a governing force, of any kind, behind the universe.

It has been wished, and wished again, that the universe could hold perfect moments in perfect memory, the clearest remembrance of things left behind. Alas this form of memory is not possible. The camera of the universe affects the actions therein. The ultimate quantum cat scenario, the fates of all mankind walking a quantum plank from a multi-universal ship, blindfolded and screaming for release…or so it seems to certain flawed observers.

John is walking, ostensibly, hand in hand with a beautiful woman he calls Maggie. John is, without a perfect camera, a perfect book to scribble him down in, an attractive man walking with an attractive woman. They, if it can be reliably reported, speak nothing of the office. The straggling passersby, an even more untrustworthy set, nod to him; the straggling passersby do not see them at all.

They, if this is to be believed, are walking to a certain store of sundries. They, if this is a true narrative, are to peruse vagaries and nick-knacks under the auspices of purchase. They arrive to find a door covered in plywood, a plank of heavier wood affixed across its center.

Maggie speaks with empathetic tones, "Oh, poor Cassiel! He must have had to shut down!"

Maggie is glowing in John's eyes, her sympathy a vision from somewhere lost within him.

John mumbles back indistinctly about Cassiel telling him something about money troubles. John grasps the air near his waist, miming a comforting squeeze. He recalls a half-forgotten time in the basement of the shop, the shelves toppled over, the stock strewn across the floor, the floors sticky with neglect. He thinks it must have been when the shop first opened, yet to be organized.

"You would have liked my father, you know?" Maggie says out of nowhere, breaking John from his mumbling revelry.

"Would I have?"

"Yes. Before he fell ill, he had this habit of half listening and responding back with mumbles. But when you questioned him about it, he could recite book, chapter, verse of whatever it is you were talking about; like he had a split in his mind where he lived in one half and existed in the world with the other. You're like that at times."

"Wouldn't that mean we'd ignore each other and live in our own worlds?"

"Yes. I think you two would have had very nice and quiet walks together, never bothering the other with trifling things, like conversation or directions. You would be simply two dreamers in a wood, making up stories for the void."

"Sounds nice, I wish we had met and gotten in some walks before it got too bad."

"The getting too bad is what I'm concerned with. I'm afraid one day you will start to mumble like him and never return from that half of your head. I don't want to watch that again, John."

"You won't have to. I'm fine. It's nothing to worry over; been like this since…well, since childhood. I'll always come home in the end."

"Good. See that you do." She lightly punches him on the arm on the way to locking elbows.

They continue on past the shops and into that shapeless country ever full of untold stories. If the camera of the universe were perfect, and tuned in correctly, it would see him disappear into the darkness of the back streets, happily holding hands, happily whistling a wordless song.

# 19. The girl from Ipanema.

The office often reminds John of elevator music.

At times, he sits and watches Kali as she hums tunelessly, her hands moving languidly across a rusting typewriter.

Hephaestus often enters, and demands from her a dance about the room. In those moments, the record player is dragged in from wherever it currently exists. The record player is an imitation of an old Victrola, its massive horn jutting out uncomfortably into the vibrating air. John will sit and watch, in good times like these, the giant and the waif move with practiced skill. The iron of the ceiling fans will reflect like candelabra, diffusing light in wheezing sparkles through the particulate air. The dance will only last one song, no more, no less. Hephaestus will bow deeply as Kali curtsies. John will sit and watch, feeling like this has played out before.

It all reminds him of elevator music.

In one such time, the iron fan blades are moving papers with no discretion, while the record player sits quietly. Hephaestus turns from his dance, and with demanding eyes, forces the attention of John.

”John, I would ask that you join me for a moment. It's a matter of some import.”

“Of course.”

They move from the now silent Victrola and the silent Kali, in the front room, of couches and past-tense mysteries.

“First, and this is the least important part, as far at time is concerned, I must give you yet another book."

He leans across the carpeted void to hand John a book. On its cover the fading words 'Dispatches From the Periphery' can be discerned.

"Please read this at a time of peril. These words will wake you from the vertigo of looking too deeply."

"I'm sorry, when shall I read it?"

"You will know when it is time, time being a malleable term. I remember the clay tablets on which we first learned to press awareness into descriptive. I recall our feeble attempts to chisel into the world something to pass along our perceptions, to move adjectives down through the generations. I still smell the ink wafting from drying scrolls. The world was simpler then: no computers, no Internet, no immediacy. I miss it dearly."

"You miss scrolls?"

"It is of no importance. I am sorry to have forced you to listen to my nostalgic rambling. John, I sit you here so we may talk of your past, and the tiny heresies harbored within," Hephaestus smiles at him like a cartoon snake.

"What heresies do you speak of? My life, although not chaste by any means, hasn't been marred by anything as dramatic as heresy."

"The heresy I refer to is your brother."

As they speak the house shifts on its foundation. It knows the importance of the scene being played out within. The house knows of the schism in both of them, of the growing want for reprieve from weight carried for too long.

"That is not up for discussion." he growls. "The past is exactly that."

"Well, John my boy, you don't have to speak. Leave the

speaking to your friend and manager Hephaestus James Bonobus. Let us start with the significant part. Your brother died while under your guard."

He is perplexed at Hephaestus' knowledge of his past, "Sir, honestly, this doesn't have much to do with what we do here."

The house warms. The people within wait, *in situ*. This has played here before, and will again, with ever-changing faces and plastic stakes. The bridges in the mind cross and mend.

"What do you know of the work done here?"

For the first time, John sees anger within the giant.

"John," Hephaestus roars, "you are a minuscule cog in a much larger machine, a machine for which a purpose has yet to be found. For now, if you can please give me leave, I should like to find out what you learned from that day; what was taken away from the disaster that left your brother broken and you, presumably, as well."

John sinks into his seat, sighing in realization that he has been waiting for this moment, that he has been wishing for a forceful confrontation with his past.

"Please continue."

"All I have is the story of two brothers playing in a place where they did not belong, a derelict factory on an accused hill. I have the tale of a child shattered on the detritus of industry. In addition, I know that you were quiet after that; that you were brought in for help; that you shut down and learned humor; that you drew rhythmic lines in the margins of notebooks; that you created worlds to hide your anger and grief. John, you have never faced your failure as a brother, much less faced your grief at the loss of him."

John feels himself breaking, the cracks revealing his inner self, still raw and full of misery.

"Enough. That's enough."

"No. I will finish."

Inexplicably John sits quiet, ready for another emotional onslaught.

"John… I forgive you."

"What?"

"You are forgiven for the death of your brother. Children die. Mistakes are made. It is an unfortunate thing, of course, but one that is to be expected in this line of work. Now, let it go."

"Let it go? How could I let that go?"

"You have been judged for his loss. You have been blamed. You have punished yourself for these long years. Let it go John. You are forgiven."

John shatters. He breaks.

"Oh Christ…"

He runs as the start of weeping takes over his face.

He runs as Hephaestus smiles.

Hephaestus knows that the work will, indeed, be good.

## 20. Sleeping dogs.

“Maggie are you seriously telling me that I'm changing?” John sings with a light smile on his lips and a flourished gesture. “So the kid is a little weird? We watched that special together about the child who drew a detailed New York from memory. He's just like that… but with balloons… and a somewhat unsettling voice.”

Maggie nods in exaggerated agreement, “Yes! Of course that must be it! Ask the random child in your office's back yard to draw you a cityscape. We can film a sequel!”

“Yes. I'll draw up the paperwork immediately. Anyway, I'm not sure that documentaries get sequels… and, more importantly, it's just a silly job! The only change I've undergone is getting used to an early wake up and a morning walk.”

“I'm not saying you're changing. I am simply concerned that you're losing sight of what you actually have right now. You're focused on what's to come. I get the romance of this all. I get your fascination. Maggie's voice takes on a darker, more desperate tone. “I just worry that you'll forget this place, forget me.”

“I'll never forget you…wait, that came out wrong. I mean, you know I'm over the moon for you. But, also, I'm excited about the office. It's new, and weird, and magical, and, you know, kind of like home, if that makes sense at all. But, you should know, that I'm still here for you.”

“I love you too. But, I think you should take caution with the excitement. I don't know how healthy it is to work 40 hours a week at training yourself to see the world as a fake. You know?”

“Yeah, I know, but we don't call the world fake. It's incomplete, only a sliver of what is operating. At least that's what I think we teach. Either way, you're as much a part of it as I am."

They will continue like this until the apartment spins its webs.

They will go back and forth until the apartment, working as proxy for them, speaks silently in waves of peace.

Eventually, when everything is tied in a silken bow they sleep.

The galaxy spins faster, but slightly. A particle slips past an asteroid it was meant to hit. A particle freed from the whims of the blinded god embeds itself into an innocuous landscape of rolling hills dotted with cottages. The inhabitants of that landscape pay it no mind, since they have no means to comprehend such a microscopic thing.

Within that landscape a reaction is catalyzed by a small particle.

Within the landscape magma is shifted, land rises, but slightly.

Within the landscape the tectonics shift up, and up again, creating a mountain, shifting homes.

On that new landscape a mountain begins to erode into an insignificant hill, waiting patiently for new residents.

In a shared bed, asleep and entwined as only young lovers can be entwined, John and Maggie share dreams of the past, and what is to come. In a bed, in an apartment, in a town, in a space, in a universe unable to perceive itself, they sleep in comfort with the illusions of the day seeping into the unknowable reaches of the subconscious. They sleep until the blaring alarm of morning is called forth and he must rise, to don clothes and move, yet again, to an expanse of woods and a house with an indistinct nature.

## 21. Nothing like a fracas to show a man's character.

In the weeks that follow, the office works with a precision that would not be expected of a place with such plastic notions of what, exactly, it is that they do. John and Kali sit across a desk, making illegible marks on darkening paper, as if mocking the idea of language. The false letters squirm from their pens as the days drift by in a haze.

He asks questions. She responds with words that seemingly pacify, yet make no headway into understanding. They repeat actions until they are interrupted with new demands. He approaches.

Bonobus is bounding into the room.

Bonobus has eyes like prophecy.

"John the Younger! Kali! Good Morning to you both!"

John speaks, ignoring the emotions of yesterday, "Good day, Hephaestus."

"My love!" Kali bounces to him and gives a jumping hug.

"Hello to two of the most trusted in my employ. We have much work to do today, as we all know. But first, a trial of sorts. John, please follow me. We have an enemy to vanquish."

Kali looks terrified.

“Hephaestus, are you sure?”

“Yes my darling one, I am surer now than I was when I sent you down there. And you see how you turned out.”

“But I was here for months before that!”

“Some need less training. Some require more. We had no training when we found the first one so long ago. I survived.”

“Yes… but his namesake did not. And he was as experienced as they come.”

“I am aware of that.”

“John my boy, first we eat, then we move to the basement!”

Hephaestus pulls from his waistcoat pocket a velvet case. John watches as the giant’s fingers open the tiny latch upon the box.

The smell of death issues forth from the velvet box. The room fills with putrefaction.

“Oh god. Is that a part of a body?”

“Hah! Yes! It is a part of the body which lives in the yard! This, my newest friend, is the fruit of The Tree. Its smell is rather pungent at first.”

“To say the least.”

“Hah! Yes. Well, its flavor is actually rather nice. Please, before we make our way to the lower reaches let us three share a bit in convocation. Let us three taste the flesh of The Tree and celebrate our luck to be here, to be of the site.”

“I thank you Hephaestus my love.”

Kali takes up a piece of the putrid fruit and places it lightly onto John’s hand. She takes up another for herself, and for her manager.

John tries to hold back a retch as he moves the fruit towards his mouth. His eyes bulge in delight as the flavor explodes into him.

“Oh! It’s wonderful!”

"Hah! My John, always willing to jump in, both feet at once! Now, let us make haste." he places his hand gently on John's back. "Thank you for joining us Kali, we shall see you as soon as this little adventure ends."

John looks puzzled. He follows Hephaestus out of the room down the steps to the basement.

"What was that fruit?"

"It is the matured fruit of The Tree. You have tasted its more youthful form. It's much like the durian of Asia, but having other more mystical properties. My old friend, your namesake, tried the first one."

"What happened to my namesake?"

"He lost sight of an enemy. John, you must understand that you could lose your life here today. Or lose, at least, a facsimile thereof. However, I believe you will conquer. All you need to do is use the sight that stunned the birds and stained the sky. If you see that way, you will thrive."

"What? I don't even know who our enemies are, or how to fight them… and I don't have a weapon."

"The enemy, today, is an it. It is a member of an unnatural order. You fight it the way you unintentionally fought the birds. Your sight is your weapon. You will understand when you enter. If you do not, you fail."

"But, why am I fighting it? What did it do to us?"

"They destroyed the previous world by invading this one. They took the perception of the one who previously held your name; they left him a snarling vicious thing until he was taken below the ground. They killed many before we founded this place and developed the perception to send them away. Those things can see our world for what it appears to be to the non-sighted. They hate the non-sighted. They are offended by their scent; their look, or something else intangible to our senses. Our purpose has always been to hunt down the things before they hunt the unknowing innocents. They live in the periphery, in that small space of half sight. They live in the spot where we are training you to look."

"But they have done nothing to me at all, I've never heard of a thing like that killing anyone. And I don't even know who my namesake was. I've only had this name for a few weeks."

"You hear it all the time! You just haven't been able to perceive it as such. I can show you thousands of examples of their vicious attacks; where you see newsprint and television, we see reports of slaughter and a river of violence running into the periphery. And, let us not forget, they destroyed your namesake, your ancestor, John the Elder…"

Hephaestus James Bonobus screams out from the inner most depths of his being. His pain made vocal. "Never forget the one who gave you his name! Never forget what caused this polluted mess!"

"I didn't forget! I never knew. Hephaestus, I never knew him. Mr. Bonobus I'm not informed enough for this, yet." John's voice slips into more and more passive tones. In a dulcet voice he pleadingly asks. "How can I risk my life for something I've never actually seen?"

"Thank you for your patience, John the Younger. Your power here often overwhelms us, the walking marionettes of your periphery. Please, think about it this way: if you believe there is nothing there, that there is no denizen of the other side, it cannot hurt you. If you perceive the truth of the situation, then it cannot hurt you, for it fears our kind. They are hurt by our perception of their true nature. So, John the Younger, your time here will end unless you enter, and decide the end of this day. And decide you will."

"Hephaestus, I don't want to leave."

"I know. You can see the situation, but not all of it yet. Enter. I will be here when you are victorious. Remember the spaces you looked between to see The Tree, the birds, and the sky for what they truly are."

"I just try to perceive that same thing I saw when the birds fell and The Tree moved? It can't be that simple."

"Of course it's that simple, John the Younger. The one thing I am not is a liar. I swear to you, as someone much wiser in the ways of things, you will not come to harm if you see properly. Walk into that darkness, John, and look upon that space with the eyes we have nurtured together."

"Good. This makes sense. If there is nothing there, as one part of me sees, nothing can hurt me. If you are correct, and there is something malevolent there to see, I have the skills to beat it back. What the hell; logic is logic. I'm in."

"No. Logic is not logic, but that will become clear later. I will be out here upon your return. I wish you a good battle, John."

"Thank you Hephaestus. I'm banking on you being correct here. I guess I'll see you after it's over."

"Indeed."

John has learned, since his arrival, to look past tautology and contradiction, to embrace the intangible. He looks to the door, it shimmers, a contiguous line drawing of flowers and crop circles appear.

Hephaestus holds back a laugh, knowing the nascent abilities in his presence.

John tests the handle.

It gives to his turn.

The light inside is low, the room fogged to the point of solidity. Framed by the doorway, he turns his head back to Hephaestus.

"How am I supposed to see in there?"

Hephaestus smiles broadly, "You better figure that out before it does."

He shoves John into the room and slams the door behind him. Taking out a half-smoked cigar from his pocket, humming a wordless song, the fat-man sits in a chair across the hall from the door. The smoke begins to circle him in rough shapes, humans and birds created and destroyed as motes of dust pirouette in the cigar air.

John walks in thick fog. The air is dry, yet the room spirals in fog and shadows. The room is all outlines, fragments of monochromatic lines in a sea of nothing. He knocks into a chair, steadying it with his trembling hand. He nearly tumbles as he enters an area of room be-rugged in heavy shag; he trips into another chair and laments the frequency of furniture.

He hears a scuttling.

In fear, he jerks his head towards the noise.

In darkness, there is the sense of movement.

In the darkness, he lifts the chair into an imitation of a lion tamer. In his terror, he finds pause to smile at his idiot circus posing. More noises echo through him as he searches with motions of his head. A shadow skims across the floor, too fast and fluid for his eyes to register.

He looks desperately into the ethereal smoke for any visual purchase, finding none. John breathes in a deep pull of air, calming his shattered nerves as best he can. His heartbeat slows mildly as his breathing grows more regular. He looks to the seat, held comically in front of his chest.

It attacks.

It exists, at that moment, as a liquid shadow, pure motion not yet having substance. From that shadow a form takes shape hurling itself onto John, the chair knocked from his hands. He falls, with the shapeless horror mounted on him. John's hands find purchase on what would be a neck, if such words could be ascribed to this darkened fog. He presses with all his strength, fighting against fangs, or so he would call them fangs for lack of a better word. It is then that John makes the realization of the inner transparency of the monster. He sees this shadow as a break in the trees, a glimpse of something unnatural. He remembers what Kali told him about seeing the birds. He remembers the sky, the birds falling, the panicked run, her glowing, his relief, the sense of staring into something new. He looks up at the creature and lets go his effort, dropping his hands.

Now a yelp, and a wavering in the animal's shape.

The shadow thing becomes something familiar, but thoroughly new. A homunculus of tumorous growths with a human-like face sits where once there was shadow. A dog-shaped form, mutated, ugly, shivers upon the concrete, impotent under the duress of his vision.

John stands, shifting his vision back to what he knew as life the week before. The thing lifts up what could be called its head, turning back into the darkened ephemeral canine of the moment before. He looks back to the thing with pity, and through the periphery it squeals, falling upon the floor. The room is clear of fog, radiant. The creature lays motionless in a far corner, it is smaller now, disgusting and harmless.

John sees greenhouse enclosures, the remains of the chair. He walks over to the creature and picks it up by the scruff. He turns back to see Hephaestus in a chair smoking. John lofts the cancerous thing at him. Hephaestus's massive chest contracts with the impact.

"I need a cookie," John walks past Hephaestus proclaiming over his shoulder. "Also, I broke your chair."

## 22. The Lovers(torn).

In the darkening skies of his walk home, John kills no birds, no incorporeal canines.

In the darkening skies of his walk home, John talks to himself about foggy fights and his disintegrating sanity.

He thinks of Maggie, longing for her to be by his side. He thinks of Maggie and wonders if she will ever understand the nature of his new path. He walks under the darkening sky as the fight in the basement begins to slip into memory.

He arrives at the facade of a dying building, and climbs the steps leading into what was once his safe haven from a world unfit for him. Now, he walks from those steps into a waiting Maggie, her eyes burning with a mix of fury and anxiety.

He starts to tell her of his fight with the thing in the cellar. He regales her with sweeping gestures to indicate birds, and low movements to show a canine stride. He paces and sweats. His voice rises and drops with practiced drama. He starts to tell her of his new found wonder. She begins to see that her life with John will soon be over.

“I can't listen to this anymore! I cannot sit and listen to you crumble. You need serious fucking help.”

Maggie is less than enthused with the story John has told her. She cannot understand phantom chairs, balloon children, and dogs that are not dogs.

"Well, maybe you can try to fucking support me in my endeavors for once!"

“John. This isn’t something to support. This is a mental breakdown in the form of an office in the woods. John, you know you are predisposed to this. You need help.”

"Christ. Yeah, I need help. That's always your solution. Why can't I have a religious experience? Why can't my life be revelatory for once?"

"Because you're talking about killing animals in the basement of your office, not finding Jesus. Can't you see the difference?”

"Fine. Fine. But I'm telling you, it happened. Jesus or not."

"It's fucking peculiar John. Odd. Nonsense. Impure.”

“I know it sounds odd, but hear me out… I saw the thing, both as animal and something else. I mean, wait, allow me to look at you that way. It didn't hurt Kali when I did it.”

He reaches for her face, to mimic his interactions with Kali.

“No. You will not. And you can look at that girl all you want. I'm fucking done here. Go feed your demon trees, I can’t be around for this again. I cannot sit here and watch you fall apart.”

Maggie has slammed the door as John sits down at the table. An untouched meal sits as a reminder of her existence. He decides that the local pub is a better option than cold tacos and introspection.

## 23. Sometimes, even the beatified need a drink.

The pub at the end of the street.

The pub which he has, years previously, drank away evenings singing with women and yelling with friends.

He enters, despondent. To him, the room looks the perfect shade of dark. To him, the bar's wood paneled decor is the exact companion for him on a night like this.

"Whiskey, neat. Beer chaser."

The bartender nods in that bartender-y way, a recognition of lost women and other painful errata. The saddened one watches a careful pour and thanks the nameless man who provides the liquid.

"I didn't know this place reopened." John questions, not caring about an answer. He is filling the void with noise, blocking his thoughts of the events of the day.

"Reopened? Been here as long as I can remember."

The bartender is uninterested with John. The bartender is wavering slightly in the metaphysical wake of this moment.

"Oh, I could have sworn this got shut down… no matter really. Just making conversation I suppose."

"I get the idea. We all move at the speed beholden to the path. Can't just decide to take in the whole world in one fell swoop, that's libel to make you go a little crazy."

The bartender looks younger than before.

John nods, feeling at home in the empty room.

“But,” the middle aged man continues, “I suppose trying is all we have to hang our hats on. I figure as long as you're still upright, and you keep your eyes open… just enough… you can get through this place." The bartender gestures broadly to the empty bar.

John coughs on invisible dust.

"That sounds good to me, tomorrow. For now, I think I will drink and feel sorry for myself. I will see how the light affects my eyes in the morning. Cheers."

As John perceives it, his beer turns to a swirling mass of faces, laughing, falling, screaming, cascading in the dying foam like carnival rides and LSD.

As the world perceives it, his demeanor moves from depressed and alone to frightened and anxious. He places his beer back down and sighs heavily, finding this normal for the last few weeks of his life. He decides the decidedly non-demonic whiskey shot may prove a more fruitful endeavor. It screams in pain as he attempts to drink from the brown liquid.

He stares into the whiskey, searching for a mouth, vocal chords, or any other sign that his head did not invent a scream. He sees no means of vocalization. He sees no sense in the day that has transpired.

That's enough, he thinks, deciding that escape may prove more sensible than falling into further alcohol traps. He throws uncounted money on the bar and stands with obvious purpose.

"Thanks. I must be going."

"No problem. Good evening, young master."

John half jogs to the door, and out, walking straight into the massive shape of Hephaestus James Bonobus. He is surprised at the relief he feels seeing the behemoth.

"Hephaestus?"

“John the Younger, I hope upon hope that no alcohol has touched your lips this day.”

“No, I didn't feel much like drinking.”

“Please, no more lies. We will be open from now on. I promised you answers to your questions, and now they will be given. Consider this the third day. Join me for a brandy.”

“I don't know that I feel like drinking right now.”

“Of course you do, that's why we build these places. You have yet to see how this works. Please, trust your new father. No more faces and demons in the bubbles.”

“How did you…?”

John has lost the urge to question. He will follow the large man's lead for the evening. Reentering the pub, the bartender screams.

“Hephaestus! Welcome most esteemed customer and proprietor! I had no idea he was with us. I will immediately provide brandy and peanuts. Your table is now existent, please, please, join us in comfort.”

They take drinks and sit at a table in the back corner, shrouded from the light of the main section of the bar top. They sit as the light shifts to that familiar office sepia.

John, dissolute, stares at his drink, glowing, radiant.

“I have no idea what is going on anymore. The office did this to me. Please. I have no specific questions anymore. However, I have multiple pages of them written in the apartment. Please tell me this will be okay, or that I am unfit for the position. I think I need what this job is showing me. But it’s making Maggie leave. I need her. Either I've finally gone insane, or there is something else operating here. Hephaestus, please, just tell me what’s happening.”

“John… the Younger. Do you know why you have your

name?"

"You've mentioned a predecessor. Though, Maggie thinks it's because you had a book with that name in it already and reused it for me."

Hephaestus roars with laughter, the brandy forms circles in its wake.

"She is a perceptive one! Well, that is the answer… but far from the solution. We wrote that book years before we knew you, years before your birth. You see, we know our potential employees well before they become able to be so. I gave you that book, and that name, because I was shown that you may be able to be in my employ. The Child tells me you see better than he's seen in many years. He, having been in this company for longer than I, is someone I trust."

"How long have you been with this company? Honestly this time. I know the child cannot be more than 12, yet Kali tells me he has seen over 30 years with the firm. This has to be some kind of long form joke that I'm not getting."

"Yes. This is some kind of joke. I described it the same way when I founded the firm, many more years ago than I count for this body. You see the joke is that most cannot see the joke, the operative principle of the goings on around us. We hire those with the potential to see the joke, to see the periphery. You can see my fish; the enemies of the way to the back door. You can see properly without much effort or learning. Most can see if aware enough, but it takes years, decades. We cultivate those that can become aware enough for use. Your initial training is over, or so I assume by your untouched drinks on your way out… you saw the faces, you stunned the birds and danced with the periphery in the basement. You are part of us already."

"What does that mean? I think I can somewhat control this vision at times, but I don't understand what it is that I'm seeing. What was that thing?"

"That thing was a vision from the other place, the world that was."

"I've heard that phrase before. You said you'd answer me."

"I will answer all, but some answers can only come later. I am sure there will be a later between us."

"This is too much. Can I ask a simple one?"

"I said I can answer all that you can listen to."

"Why can I drink Brandy?" Hephaestus laughs. The tension seems abated. John seems to trust this situation.

"Because, my newest friend… brandy was made for people like us. Now, let us lift drinks and spirits… there is much to discuss."

## 24. Iterations in the dark.

In the darkness of the yard, The Child and Kali sit on dew-covered grass. They, like stone Buddhas, sit unmoving under a great tree.

In the darkness of the yard the smell of moldering leaves and the faint whispers of autumn flavor the air.

In the darkness of the yard, the archetypal forms of a child and a girl speak as elders.

"Child, do you recall how you died?"

"Girl, I do recall this. Do you recall the last time we went through this place?"

"I do. We spoke in ancient languages and answered to forgotten names. I think fondly of those that we once were."

"I think on them fondly as well. To see us die again, and again, is something too much to ask of such entropic husks."

"You speak wisdom. The Tree will fruit soon."

"He will die soon."

"The motions are their own. We move because of those simple forces set to work so long ago."

"We move as reaction to that which was done to this place."

"Child, I should like for you to look into my eyes again. Let us celebrate the uncertainty which we know exists in these trivial decisions."

"Girl, I will look upon you with the vision of our former selves. Let us find a room with electric light and join in convocation."

"So it was. So shall it be."

With alternating shapes, and motions they move from place to place, to take communion in the name of what was and will be. They exist, for that moment, both as past and present, as realized and unrealized, as Newton and Quantum, simultaneously alive and dead. They exist(ed).

## 25. Libations.

Meanwhile, in a theoretical pub on the edge of a maybe-town, a giant and a young man sit.

In that theoretical pub, they speak with Latinate roots and Germanic grammars.

In that theoretical bar, they raise glasses to the void.

They drink. This is not a simple thing. Hephaestus drinks like it were the entirety of life condensed into small glasses. John stares at emptying glasses, fighting back the drunken forces of revelry.

Hephaestus speaks like water, gesticulating wildly, drawing figures in the air, drafting geometry in the spaces between words. At times, he leaves few pauses, and in others, he leaves voids and oceans in which to think and respond.

In one of those chasms, John chooses to speak.

"I don't feel guilty."

"My, what a fine statement."

"I thought I'd feel guilty right now, but instead I'm drunk and having a good night. My life is broken. Maggie is gone. I have no idea what I do for work. I have no idea what is going on with birds and dogs. Everything is terrible by any accounting, yet I feel somewhat content. No more guilt than I had yesterday, if yesterday even happened."

"Yes, yes, I'm so glad you said that. John the Younger has never been, in all his incarnations, an alcoholic, but in most, a drunk. It's a wonder it took you all so long to figure this out."

Hephaestus smiles and turns to the bar. The barkeep prepares more drinks. John looks to Hephaestus in anticipatory silence. The bartender leaves a bottle, a bucket of ice, and a jar of peanuts on the table.

"John, let me illuminate a few things for you. The HJ Bonobus Corp was founded by someone much like myself… so much so I call him me. We are an older thing in possession of the words of something even older. We can see, you included, into the world that was, the world that sits upon the periphery. It is gone to most people now, leaving in its stead the yellowing wasteland you've seen glimpses of. It will become perfect again, in union with the world of frontal vision, the world that you've known."

"Are we a religious sect?"

"Oh, lord no. We are simply the last few human denizens of the periphery. We are the heralds of a better day where we all can return to where we belong. For now, we feed the Trees and make grand circles. Think of the world you have previously perceived as a prism, pure, white light enters and is refracted. The world is a splintering refraction of something more pure, more complete. The periphery is something closer to the source. It is the world as perceived without a prism. It is the world as observed with the notion in place that true observation is impossible."

"Sounds like one of those Masonic conspiracy theories. Next you'll tell me we run the illuminati."

"Alas not, those groups exists purely in frontal vision. It is often that imagination mimics what we can see, though falsely. We're no more religious than that pestering notion at the back of your spine when you're about to get punched, or the lingering electrons after a kiss."

"I'm beginning to see the shape of it. Nevertheless, it's still vague; it still feels without actual substance, like air, or lunacy. Let me ask you one more thing."

"I promised answers."

"Can we have another drink?"

The fat man's laugh echoes through the empty bar. John begins to understand that he will soon, if all goes to plan, be very, very drunk.

## 26. The Universe.

The Tree is almost finished, beckoning to Hephaestus to join it again. The pulsing of the ground is exponential; root systems feel the change approaching as limbs move in sync.

Hephaestus looks on from the balcony watching John and The Child mill about the yard, drawing figures in the dying grass.

To Hephaestus, John is a glowing pillar, a wild flame of light and imagination.

To Hephaestus, John is himself as a younger man.

To John, Hephaestus is an aged version of himself overlaid on top of a construct of father.

To the perspective of Hephaestus, The Child is as he once was, reclaiming a lost aspect through the imagination of John.

Hephaestus sees them as the incarnate future, the way that things will be when set right; He sees in them the future, the fissure closed, the scars healed.

From his balcony, he sees that The Child has come to the same conclusions about John. The time of the old pairings is ending. He wonders, if one such as him can still wonder, how John sees all of this. He wonders how he, as a proxy father, can make this transition go any smoother. The smell of ancient charcoal and smoke is in the air.

Hephaestus remembers the days of new religion, new beliefs, in "The Burned-Over District" of his earlier years. If one such as him could reminisce, he would be waxing philosophic about that place and the inventions therein. However, one such as him, one invented by a time and a person long gone, does not reminisce often. Hephaestus breathes deeply from artificial memory, grinning as The Child below prepares the meal.

In the yard, as sure of a location as one gets in a world of half perceptions and moving fables, John feels compelled to watch the Keeper of The Tree do his work. The child, with his balloons, now appears as an adult, through the lens of the periphery. His eyes are radiant, his face flawless, angelic in its aspect. John, content in this moment, in the comforts of this sideways universe, sits and watches with relaxed vision.

It is then that he sees what The Child holds.

It is then that John recoils from the balloons.

What was seconds previous a balloon floating in the intermediate area between ground and sky, a childhood token of love and innocence, is now a naked, jaundiced, hairless thing, writhing on a bloodied cord.

It looks wrong, not meant for this world, for those eyes.

It looks as if created for another environment, another planet entirely, ejected from the subconscious of a maniac.

John feels a kinship with the horror, this reject of the universe. He notes to himself that he feels no need to approach it for further study. He has known this creature before; he has seen this heresy in dreams.

He has watched this monster from within waking nightmares.

He has run from its kin under a rain of birds.

He has battled its brother in the recesses of an office.

The Child's face is as inexpressive as John's is repulsed. Hephaestus looks on from his ivory tower, only to see John's world.

Listen.

The Child releases one of these squirming, writhing, things, and it floats through the air by some unknown aspect of physics.

It floats as if it were still a balloon.

Now, it is no mere balloon.

The doors in John's mind, now open, will no longer shut out these terrifying visions.

The screeching horror rises higher, in doing so fills John's perspective with more and more trunk, more and more tree. He follows the monster on the morbid string as it rises into the branches, if only they still were branches.

It floats into the upper reaches of The Tree.

Oh God, The Tree.

His eyes follow its transit from the base, each new inch a new horror, until the tendril branches begin their dissection.

The Tree now appears as a twisted thing, a reptilian-mammalian-chimerical monster, with a base like piles of rotting leather. The top is slowly shifting to an amorphous, bile spurting horror.

John wishes it could go back to the way it was, a nice tree in a nice yard, nothing squirming, nothing sinister. As the animal reaches the boughs, the "tree" bends forward, fast, the balloon pops.

A mist of blood rains down upon the child and the man.

A sound of cracking bone and swishing flesh mixes with the echoes of creaking branches and a slow breeze.

The branches snap back into place, the chimera becomes chameleon, again becoming tree. The Tree stops its motion as one last drip on red falls as if in lesser gravity to the abattoir grass.

John is frozen, in shock, and in blood.

John looks to The Tree, to the grass, to The Tree, to the grass, and finally to the others in the yard, shaken.

The Child smiles broadly. “You do learn quickly. The Tree saw you arrive and was nervous. It will be okay now."

John looks to the glowing form in front of him, now both man and child, and bites back a question. He knows this is something best left to another time for an explanation.

The Tree looks to John and decides on something.

John looks to what is now a child again, and a tiny hand wraps around his own, sticking together with bile and blood.

“Please. This is necessary. This is the way things circle, and again. Please.”

“I trust you, but please tell me to look away before the next feeding.”

“John the Younger,” the child speaks with a voice like gravity, “the next one will be something you need to see. The next is one of rebirth. We will feed three days hence, and remember him that will be again.”

The sway of the trees mimic the laughing of reptiles as the boy skips away. Hephaestus nods in approval from his place above. The man who is new sits down and hopes the bloody grass holds no new secrets.

## 27. The Empress(reversed).

Maggie hates heels.

She never wears heels.

Maggie, hating herself for wearing heels, locks a glass door, adorned with posters, and swivels uncomfortably on wobbling legs.

The tapping of her heels on the concrete bothers her as she zips up a jacket. She realizes that the fall is truly coming as a breeze still slightly tasting of summer blows lightly browned leaves across her path.

In the weeks since she left her apartment with John, life had found a way to move forward while simultaneously sitting stagnant.

She has twice turned back, in comfortable shoes, from that long unpaved road to John.

She has twice walked casually past the glass windows of a failed Laundromat to look up at darkened apartment windows.

She has twice felt his presence while attempting to sleep; but resolve, and the current theories of trans-locality, have prevented this notion of presence from becoming a reality.

In the weeks that Maggie has spent alone she has tried, and tried again to get over him.

In the weeks that Maggie has spent as a single young woman with the world open to her, she has dodged all flirting glances, all delicate banter.

In those weeks, she has meditated on the past, while a group of maniacs sit in a nonsensical office, dedicated to observation.

## 28. Some quality time determining philosophies.

"Hephaestus, we need to talk, if you have the time." John asks plaintively.

"Of course my boy! Please pull forth yonder seat and join me in this important convocation! I believe you are to ask me about certain animal qualities of certain childhood play toys?"

Hephaestus is giddy in his speech, bouncing with each utterance, smiling child-like with each new instance of John's confusion.

John, in turn, finds a wry smile to return. He is starting to understand the giant's sense of humor, his amusement at the workings of other minds.

"Yes, sir, the animals on the string... I don't get it. What am I seeing? Why must The Tree be fed?"

"Well, the short answer is: You cannot understand, yet. However, I am sure that you will not take that as an answer. So let me try to elaborate on the subject. You see, the dogs of arguable existence are nothing of the sort. They are simple placeholders denoting something that exists more in the periphery than in this world, or so the words would lead us to believe. The Tree takes nourishment from the minds and actions of those who can see the other side, the periphery. We scare the hounds into submission, and we feed them to The Tree. The Child hold his balloons as sacred for they represent something lost to us, each string an opportunity to regain what was lost. The ideas are bound to the string; the string is bound to the aether; and the aether is bound to this world through The Tree. When we consume its fruit, we take in the purified essence of vision, to see where the path will lead us. We can see our destination, though no part of it will be realized until arrival. And, even then, upon arrival, the destination may change its nature. I am sure that did not answer your question."

Hephaestus finishes with a flourish of a radiant smile and a half-implied bow.

John delighted, joyous, as is often the result of being in proximity to the charismatic giant, the force made flesh that is Hephaestus.

"That did not answer my question. Though, I'm beginning to understand that the further along the way of peripheral I go, the more I will have the ability to understand even further. I suppose the next logical questions are: how far does the path go? Can one leave it?"

"Well, yes and no, and all the way. It is the path of the universe, the all seeing, ever-present, camera in the sky. It is god and quantum physics. It is the path, and no more. It moves from start to end, and nowhere else. It cannot be seen unless carefully, and though a specific lens, for observation changes results. The path has been set as gospel since before gospel was spilled out in words and empty deeds. It is immutable; it is unbroken; it is perfect and unchanging; it is forever changing for that is its nature."

"Then the future is determined before hand? There is no choice?"

"No. Wrong. All there is in the universe is observation and choice, no more, no less. In essence, the choices are made before they are made. The path is from start to finish, no more, no less. It is there because it must be, though it cannot be defined by observation."

"Wait, let me get this straight… the way is set. There is a finish. But, our choices matter because the finish cannot be seen, and therefore unset. It's… well, both?"

"Hah! John, this! This is why you have come! You have worded it better than most. It is both. All you shall do is follow the path and make the proper actions and words. Eat the fruit and observe what you can. The change is simply that. Movement over time and pressures issued. We are movements on a board, not the board itself."

They sit in silence, contemplating the floor.

John is slouching like an untaut marionette.

Hephaestus balances his head on steepled fingers.

They sit in silent convocation.

Words lose more and more meaning.

## 29. Walking meditation finds the path.

The labels have been acting out of character lately.

The aspirin bottles speak of reincarnation.

The newspapers are showing pictures of death under headlines of frivolity.

John sits alone at his table staring at nothing in an attempt to process what is, to this point, unknowable.

He reads about trans-dimensional mammals devouring a wedding where a movie review should exist.

He concentrates to see words shifting from murder to joy and back again. With the heavy hand of giving up he closes the paper and returns to missing Maggie.

He taps his foot and waits for the office to open, or to be tired enough to sleep. John wonders how much a bottle of brandy costs as he turns the television on.

This wakening of electronics is a moment of significant importance. The switching of the television will turn John, previously a fan of the entertainment device, to John the Younger, sickened by what appears.

A frenetic blur of pictures and animal screech as the TV fades from black to alive. John falls back into his couch, sick, wishing for brandy or any other reprieve from this thing.

Parallel to the chaos is a smiling woman holding a box of drugs sitting sedately in pastoral bliss. He sighs again, wiping invisible things from his eyes. The woman leaves the screen and a show returns with flashing lights and screaming horrors. The lower half of the screen begins to fill with blood or bile, an unknown quantity dripping from the recesses.

John thinks of late night black and white films as the screen steadily fills with blood.

He wonders what will happen if he allows the wave to crest. Will the images on the screen become manifest? Will the putrid liquid seep into his world? Or, as he will soon decide, the screen will only be full of yet another unknown horror.

Makes sense, he thinks, everything I look at seems to die or turn to blood and ruin. He turns the once comforting thing off, wishing Maggie would return. Deciding, as is his way, that now would be a good time to wander around outside, to clear what is left of his head.

He will walk, direction-less, in hopes of gaining a kind of internal momentum.

He will walk with an angle compassed wide enough to fit his misery, the geography of being alone.

Therefore, he walks, with head tilted up, biting back tears.

His new eyes had yet to take in the stars.

Now, they are full of the light of the bygone, the potential of what came before. His knees fail him to the dirt.

He sees the stars dance in ways of destruction and creation, in swirling eddies of all things left behind and yet to be.

He stops twice to sit on the grass, wet with dew, and glowing vibrant green. This is the world as promised by Hephaestus.

This, he knows, is the truth of what must be done.

A cosmos of light against the backdrop of dark, the perception of dark, the totality eclipsed by the smaller motions of life and the universe, all orchestrate themselves in the heavenly realms.

This, he sees through watering eyes, is the love that was left when the world was how it used to be.

He bites back more tears as he lets himself think about showing this to Maggie. Again the pattern shifts from streaking white to swirling yellows and reds.

The moon seems softly laid upon the ribbon work of the night air, the stars frenetic in their energy. John is soaked in them, taken with them, in sync with all their machinations and memories.

Under those stars, he knows that his path will continue in the only way it can.

He sees himself as an automaton pressing forward with no concern for obstacle. In those stars he knows his past is but a shadow trailing in the fading light.

Under those stars, he walks to the hills; and in this revelry moves towards the site of his fracture, to the hill, and to the shadows at its apex. Without his knowledge, or forethought, he is walking to the place of dead things.

He is walking to a place where the first of many unforgivable acts took place, and will take place again if all prophecies come to pass, as they are destined to come to pass, as they are equally destined to fail.

## 30. Maggie's teapot.

This is wisdom.

She stirs her tea staring at the spirals of milk and sighs. Without John, she finds herself revisiting the places of comfort from the era before he walked into her life. Years earlier when she sat, contented with cigarettes and the revelries of youth, he had approached. She had sat unmoving as he awkwardly made advances, and she sheepishly fell forward into the waiting warms of his peculiarity.

They had spent the next years together, learning the ways of the other, learning of the light and the dark of their pasts.

Now, she finds herself seeing John's recent insanities as growing more acceptable, more in line with the subtler aspects of his character, as previously observed. As the entropic aspect of time moves her memory of them from a final spat in a small apartment, back to thoughts of laughing revelries and twisted sheets.

She is distracted from her spiraling tea meditation by the sound of an engine grinding, bellowing in the night.

She finds herself less confident in her assertions, her decision to leave. John was a force in her adult existence; as with any force an equal yet opposite. In the case of John, his equivalent force was made of creative insanities and a slight history of mental issues.

She thinks as the engine outside is silenced, that her anger is starting to abate.

She debates walking into that same revelry state which had twice tempted her into reunion.

She thinks the comforts of increasing novelty drawing her back are to be ignored until they cease.

She thinks it is best to forget the comforts of John the Younger, nee Weishaupt.

Maggie has no idea that a play is about to take place, repeating the story of a singular evening years previous.

She does not hear the door open behind her.

She does not hear the paradoxically light footsteps approach her table.

She does, however, hear the paradoxically mellifluous greeting of a giant.

"You, my loveliest one, must be Margaret Anne. May I share your table?"

His approach is without threat, his demeanor familiar in its exacting oddness. She looks up, startled, and beholds the antediluvian spectacle before her. A nearly seven feet tall man with tailored 18$^{th}$ Century garb, complete with pocket watch in hand, chain pulled taut, stands over the diminutive girl still spinning milk spirals in ever colder tea.

"You may, assuming you tell me how you came to know my name? Credit collector?"

His laugh shook the room, "No, no, far from it. I am Hephaestus James Bonobus of the HJ Bonobus Corp. We have newly acquired a promising worker called, formally, John the Younger. I believe you are familiar with this man?"

"Ah, the fat man makes his entrance. John told me about you."

"Yes, my dearest, I am, as you so put it, the fat man. John sends his greetings, though he does not know it. I should like to explain to you a little of our business if you are so inclined to listen."

“By my estimation I have two cups of tea left. You have exactly that long to convince me.”

“I should expect we'll have remainders, should my assumptions prove correct.”

The teapot is lifted; the ceremony begins; the conversation starts in earnest. If she were the type to stare into teacups while conversing, the spiraling shapes would appear as faces in rotation. His eyes meet hers as the rotund professor turns into carnival barker, into pitchman.

Maggie sits and listens to each salvo, responding in kind.

He sweats and waves frantically.

She begins to smile through the spaces between. She sees in him a flirt, a giant, a genius and a man with no ill intent. He sees her fall to his vocalizations, her eyes in sync with his own. She opens herself, and he glows with the inner warmth familiar to the seers of the periphery.

Maggie is drawn to him, as if he possesses the answers to questions not yet articulated. She feels herself beginning to understand John's trust and adoration of the man.

They laugh until a server asks them to leave, the other tables having found themselves covered in upside down chairs.

In the dark, he walks her home, an apartment not far from the main cluster of shops in the town.

In the night he feels the duty is done, the seeds of idea firmly planted.

Standing in front of her door, she feels the charm of this man is something to be considered from afar, his scent too pervasive in the crawling air.

She is reminded of crushes on professors and stubble of her father.

She wishes him good evening, trying to draw deep breaths to stop her swooning. She knows what John must see in him.

As Maggie readies for bed she realizes that the fat man has the same smell as John.

She looks out of her window towards the hills knowing she misses John and the feeling of completeness he brings to a room.

In the dreary evening, she knows she will see him again.

In sheets, clean and warm, she knows that somehow this is all the way it is meant to be.

# 31. The Tower (on the hill).

John walks with disinterest in direction.

He is entranced with constellations and the mad, radiant, shapeless masses darting between.

He is hypnotized by the trees he walks along side. The trees, for their part, seem happier for the company, content in the presence of one who knows them so well.

The incline of his walk arrests his revelry, the slope changing from gradual to significant. John imagines leaning forward against the slope and gravity. He pictures himself in a wind tunnel, ever pressing forward against the forces put before him.

He has made it to the hills past the town; past the pond, past the fields. He walks past the impossible places he hid as a child. He walks beyond the swath of woods that cradled him as a child, broken, alone with his grief and guilt. He walks past the momentary mistakes of the years before, and the mistake he is learning to leave behind.

He sees a lone leaf falling and follows its progress towards the earth. This leaf, in its swinging chaos of gravity shakes him from his perverse nostalgia. Looking up the inclined street to the outline of the old factory, he shivers in the still-warm evening. He realizes where he finds himself.

It has been a dilapidated shell since before John was born. During his childhood, this was a place of shadows and horror, the place of ghosts and the fearful midnight entries of the braver children. In his youth, it was the site of great tragedy. The screams of his parents are now echoes mixed with thunder and the then ubiquitous sirens.

John does not know that he was walking towards an office much like the one he currently works in. What John does not know is that the place is, in fact, a location of past horrors and still healing wounds. It is a place left to rot by people much like him, a place of dead things, an office devoid of purpose.

He looks to the building feeling an unknown dread. He looks to the artifice, the symbol of his fall, and for the first time since his mistake, approaches the gates of this emptiness. Scanning for the section of rusted fence he recalled from his youth, bent up to allow the secret comings and goings of the local youth. Deciding to explore this feeling, he crouches and shimmies through the hole in the fence. His shirt catches and rips, continuing as his skin becomes subtle red as seen through torn fabric.

He is overtaken with nausea; with his approach, his life is manifest in his bowels, churning, acidic.

He knows this place.

He recognizes it as part of the periphery, part of his new covenant.

Looking, without peripheral awareness, it seems to him a familiar dilapidation, the same rusted metals and broken stone as once back dropped his childhood. With the vision born of the ancient world, of the periphery, he sees heartbreak.

And so from the periphery he sees a place of broken things, a place in desperate need of mending.

He sees the intersection of his realities, the past mistakes, the past redemption and the future of the seeing. John walks into the nexus of his being, the bloodstains below the surface.

He walks to the facade of the things now left behind.

He is joined with the past pairing through blood and through perception.

He approaches the front door steadfastly hanging onto its one intact hinge. He tries the handle, knowing it would be locked, and more so that the lock would be ineffective at halting his entry. The door swings open, with rusting protest, on its one operational hinge, holding an impossible angle. It falls to the floor, and he is awash in a flurry of dust.

After a fit of coughing, he perceives a cacophony of smell and sight, of chaos and the feeling of discomfort, a wave of something screaming ‘unwelcome’. John, squinting against the dust, tries to make out any form inside. He sees the floor writhe as if covered in snakes moving in dark water.

The dust now settling allows him to make out the layout of the room, the floor crawling with insects. He steps inside focusing his sight to see a dusty room, with no place for snakes or the various hidden monsters of the periphery. Stepping forward slowly allowing his eyes to adjust to the dark room, seeing only shapes barely discernible as variances in the darkness. From that darker place a swirling mass of energy assails him, erupting in a wave of blue and black, shapeless. The wave of energy hits John's chest with terrible velocity and force. Thrown back through the doorway and over the steps, he lands harshly on the industry-laden ground.

He is now lying, bewildered and bleeding, upon a pile of rusted wires and powdering concrete. He moans softly as he turns to his side looking back into that awful portal.

"What the hell was that?"

Somewhere inside him, he knows the answer. Something within him recognizes the power existent here. The Trees shiver in recognition. He knows this place holds significance. He knows he is not welcome in this dead place upon the hill. He knows that he must consult Hephaestus about this place. John knows that he will return here, for good or ill.

## 32. This universe, according to Richard Brautigan.

As John walks away from the factory, his head still throbs from his encounter upon the hill.

He thinks of his brother, and the steady ache of his loss. He thinks of college, and the comforts of new books.

He thinks of Brautigan's "Trout Fishing in America."

"Trout Fishing in America" showed him a secret world of metaphors made flesh. Brautigan introduced him to the idea of non-local consciousness as character.

John walks down a hill thinking of college and the notions gained and lost therein.

John juggles the idea of a metaphor as a character. He thinks of his new office, of his new coworkers.

He thinks of "Trout Fishing in America", and its journey through the various places of his imagination.

He thinks of the place in the woods and draws metaphors in the air. The air turns cool as he steadily moves downhill, towards memories of "Trout Fishing in America."

Trout Fishing in Implied Universes walks down a steady incline. Its head is filled with unknown thoughts and oddly formed energies.

Trout Fishing in Implied Universes feels an earthquake in each step. Its vision shakes as its left foot falls; its vision blurs with the landing of the right.

Trout Fishing in Implied Universes' head rings with the

echoing noise of earthquake footsteps on a downward path. Its brain is reordering itself to take in yet another reality, one whose cornerstone is set upon an accursed hill.

Trout Fishing in Implied Universes walks down an earthquake hill and throws out ideas into the darkness. It reels in forms and structures, lies and unbridled truths. It walks downhill, falling to pieces under its seismic steps, towards an older reality, yet new to his vision.

Trout Fishing in Implied Universes shakes violently as it moves with robotic motions towards an old house in a half-old forest.

Trout Fishing in Implied Universes' motions mimic a writhing which is happening simultaneously across town. Its nature being redefined, like rebuilding after a storm.

## 33. What do you mean he's dead?

“Wait. What do you mean he's dead?” John's face is slowing going slack. What was at first a strange comment in a series of others is slowly turning into something more prosaic and painful.

“We found him this morning in the bedroom above the doors, happy in permanent sleep. I'm sure he'd have wanted you there, but death is a funny thing sometimes.”

“Dead, dead? Like not alive, breathing ceased, brain function over, dead?”

The house shutters as John stammers in recognition.

“Dead dead.” Kali is using the most somber of tones. “I'm sorry to have to hurt your feelings John the Younger, but this sort of thing happens all the time. We are all essentially dead, just waiting to be actualized; look more carefully, you will see it. Would you like to sit with him before we proceed?”

John nods and they hold hands, walking through what yesterday was a wall.

In a room that John has never been in, an unbelievably round thing lying still on a bed. He stares at the body in silence. The house shutters as he sits besides the once vital man.

John has not been around a dead person since the funeral of his grandmother. She was older, caked in stage paint, and far less rotund. His eyes well up, his back shakes slightly in the fight against breakdown. He looks into the world that this giant has shown him.

On the bed lies the body of a child, its eyes fixed open, and on the mouth a subtle, knowing, smirk of accomplishment. This makes John forget his horror for a moment and smile at this stilled grotesque.

Kali places her hand, small and gentle, upon John's back, "I believe we have an appointment with The Tree. I feel that you know grieving is a thing best left to the other place."

## 34. Since he's not here to tell it.

Let us be plain for a second. Hephaestus is dead.

We know; it is a shock.

We were shocked the first time as well.

However, what is done is done.

You may be asking yourself, who are 'We'?

We have no idea, actually.

Talking camera, alternate incarnation of the nameless narrator, or a flaw in the observation, it is unimportant.

Indeed, what is done is done.

What is buried will remain buried until such time that the Trees of reality grow forth and unite what is past with what is present. This, strangely enough, is coupled with the forces of life and death, both physical and mental. The head moves into The Tree as The Tree grows into the head, both metaphorically and in reality(If there can be one reality as agreed upon by the disparate majorities floating here and there). The bodies become the Trees, and the Trees make fruit to feed to the bodies only for the head to turn into something which will see The Tree for the truth of it, in time to be consumed, yet again.

Moments before a body moved through an office in the woods, a single photon, from a far-off star, was slamming forcefully into a cluster of cells on a primitive planet. That star has watched our story previously. That cluster of cells reacted faster, adjusted more fruitfully. That cluster of cells, and it's near cousins lived, and thrived. That cluster of cells became the progenitor of an eye. That cluster of cells eventually allowed for a metaphorical brain stem to be a tree, in the upper reaches an organ capable of existing while both open and closed.

The Tree, as a powerful metaphor for the deeper reaches of the brain has its limits. And so too the forces of the corporeal form, as shown by a giant, dead and cold in a manor house surrounded by trees of varying sentience.

Because the form dies, and because little plastic dinosaurs thrive in the smaller places, we find revelation in the coincidences as seen through the periphery. We, and by 'We', we mean the universal 'We'. The editorial 'we' can find awareness and salvation in the places only shown to those who have the skills to see.

So the little orange dinosaur, so little and spotted with rain, becomes as important as a giant tree in a false house in a wood full of dead prophets and living metaphors.

Because everything has a twin, whether here and now or old and forgotten, the world can exist and move through its epochs. Picture a snake eating its tail. Its tail exists in the past, its mouth in another dimension, and its body wavering between the two as a talisman for the people who can see. In one universe there is a joyous celebration. In another universe, a funeral is happening.

A man is sweating profusely as he drags a burden through a hoarder's maze, while, that same man quotes book, chapter, and verse eloquently. At the same moment, people are running from a maniac, as they speak beautiful elegies for the dead.

This world is simple. Opposites and twins as collided in a quantum field, as perceived by a faulty narrator over a backdrop of a system that is trying to figure itself out. The universe is an office in the woods, with a great fat man now stilled. The universe is a single step to the right of this fat man, tinted sepia and waiting for a new overlap. As it was, so it will be again, or so the best prophets and guess-men have led us to think.

## 35. A joyous ceremony at The Tree.

John walks arm in arm with Kali to the backyard, a panoply of balloons and streamers move with random gravity.

The Child and Dura sit on the grass, each holding back ascending strings. They approach in silence to match the somber hush of the gathering.

John, Dura, Child and Kali sit upon the earth, held down by random gravity. From the house, the sound of rusting hinges is heard as Hephaestus's body is carried out by unseen forces. It floats, supine, to the base of The Tree, and is slowly lowered.

The Child stands from their group, carrying a ball of twine, soaked in blood or iodine. He cuts pieces in lengths determined by his wingspan. He cuts four chords for Hephaestus' four limbs. Dura rises, walking with that aging gentility, dragging a burlap sack, wriggling behind her. Dura, with arthritic fingers opens the bag and retrieves a screaming thing… the dog creature of the basement, the food of the tree, the balloons. She, with undue elegance, ties a creature to a string, and the child does the same. John looks on, mystified.

He knows what will happen… he does not accept what will happen. The words of warning spring to his mind, *'you will not miss the next feeding, the next feeding is one of rebirth'.* They knew, he thinks; they knew this was about to happen. Kali takes his hand gently, noticing his distress.

Dura looks expectantly at the path from the road, knowing he will not come. The ropes, now tied to balloons, rise to tautness.

In the second sight the balloons scream and wail, thrash and protest.

In silence, John shutters.

In horror he is seized.

The hulking mass of Hephaestus appears now, as on the bed, a child, still, at peace.

The Child with the voice of a man walks to the front of the gathering, and addresses the audience.

The crowd murmurs in wait of his wisdom.

John waits in horror, hoping he is wrong about the scene about to unfold.

"I am the guardian of The Tree and I speak for the spirit of the man that is currently motionless and tethered in this place where he no longer belongs. I speak for the newcomers with old names and for us who have watched this before. Hephaestus was a giant of industry and power. He was a man, who in this circle, defined an office set askew, and set things right against an onslaught with the advantage of higher ground. Hephaestus is the office in the woods, as it sits now, the survivor where once there were two…"

John is beginning to understand that The Child is speaking of the place on the hill; that it holds greater significance than he had put forth. The energy John felt was something Hephaestus not only knew about, but also had experienced, firsthand. Something had happened to upset that place upon the hill, and the man who dwelt therein. Something had happened upon that hill, which Hephaestus had managed to avoid for the denizens wood.

The Child continues, "We gather to give his spirit and old form to The Tree, so that he may come again as he so chooses. John the Younger, please step forward and take from me this key, and this book."

John approaches from the makeshift crowd and takes the items from the boy that is a man.

"The book grants you the knowledge to manage this location

until a suitable replacement is given to use. The key is yours. They key represents your new dominion over the place of the hill." The crowd gasps at the utterance of the place, which has long since fallen from conversation.

"We know you found the place without instruction. We know you were repulsed without temptation. It is now your duty in the coming months to take back what we lost. My friends and colleagues, may I present to you, John the Younger, Holder of the Book, and Watcher of the Office on the Hill. Hephaestus trusted you with these things, do not disappoint him."

John touches the boy's passing shoulder and steps back into the crowd. Kali takes his elbow and kisses his cheek, whispering, "John the Younger, Holder of the Book, and Watcher of the Place on the hill, blessed are we to know you in such times!"

The boy continues as the whispers of shock die down.

"Now that we are again fully staffed and prepared for the gathering clouds, let us dispose of the shell which once was our leader and friend. Blessed be The Tree that takes our Hephaestus."

He cuts the first rope. The dead man stirs in his bonds, his left side rising.

"Blessed be the man who we loved."

He severs the second. The right side moves against the forces of gravity.

"Blessed be the seers of the periphery and the one who shows them the way."

Another, the rope across the waist, is now the only remaining tie to his previous gravity.

"And finally, blessed be this man as offering. May he return at his leisure."

The final rope is cut.

The obese body floats.

The reptile Tree waits in stillness.

The Child steps back from the platform. Kali holds John's hand.

The upper reaches of The Tree snap forward, engulfing the floating mass.

The snap of branches and bones shakes the air.

It rains upon them the wave of viscera and blood that once made up a friend and manager.

John chokes back a wretch, covered in gore, parade confetti in rain.

The Tree seems to savor the last bits, and settles back from reptile violence to subtle swaying.

"Oh God," John sits upon the grass, now red with the remains of a cast off shell. "Oh… that was… oh God."

He trembles.

"John, do not be disturbed by what you have seen. Be joyous that he rains down from above, and will nourish The Tree. He will return, as we all return. The Tree will show the way home. Now, we have work to do inside, let us shed these mourners' rags and become what we once were, again."

## 36. Afterbirth (The Fool).

John, covered in blood and chunks of gore drying in the stagnant air, enters Hephaestus' old bedroom. An indentation on the mattress exists in silent testament to his recent existence. The walls sit bare, save for the occasional scraps of yellowed newspaper tacked in random.

John sits heavily upon Bonobus' bed. He takes up the manual given to him at the ceremony, giving it a cursory glance. He places it down next to him. He rubs at his eyes. He watches the subtle movements of the walls, and the plants hanging heavy from the ceiling. He will be in charge of this place now, or one very much like it. He will be Hephaestus to some another nameless, confused, man. The canvas book sits on a desk to his right, beckoning him. He will need its words, as the time for trial will soon begin.

In the other sight, the book is leather-bound and ancient. In the other sight, it is a glowing sigil to the seers, a beacon to lead them home. In the eyes of the people of the universe, as Newton understood it, the inside cover is stark white. With John's new eyes of maybe-logic and quantum states, an inscription shows itself against the stark white:

> *It's not such an unpleasant thing, being dead. As you read, this I will be The Tree, and I will feed upon the dead. I will return from The Tree, once sated. The Child will hold his station, guardian of the sacred growth. The girl will hold her seat behind the desk, staying seated as a bringer of light. You, my son, will run this*

*place, though only in name.*

*The ruins on the hill are your charge: I expect results. Read the remainder of this document for the details, though I believe you have most of it figured out. You will speak with me soon; please do not grieve me for what I was. We all return to The Tree eventually. You will know this when you are like me... or sooner if you are not successful upon the hill.*

*Do not become enamored by increasing novelty. We know you were called to the hill. We know it threw you into revulsion. This place is yours, John the Younger. It is a place of dead trees and the failures of the generation previous. This is where you have died, and will again if you lose patience and sight... or simply succeed long enough for entropy to win. Go to the hill, and take back the place now run by the denizens of the once pure world. You will make the Trees grow again, and celebrations will be heard from the place on the hill.*

*I look forward to once again visiting you there. It is an auspicious time in the life on the HJ Bonobus Corp. We are all glad to have you along with us for it. Please move your belongings, if you so wish, into my or any other room of your choosing. This place is yours now. Hold it until such time that you shall leave. The child will show you how to tend The Tree. The Tree will show you how to rear the child. Kali is the one for whom we all wait. Do not place undue burden on her chest. Blessed are the seers, and the discoverer of lost things. Do not lose your resolve, John the Younger; we have faith in you.*

*The stars will herald your arrival,*

*-Hephaestus, ex post facto.*

John smiles through tears at the tiny writing.

“Well, that wasn't helpful at all.”

The plants nod in recognition at the final joke of a large, dead, man.

## 37. Pop music in the coming winter.

It is yet another in a growing list of abysmal Tuesdays. Maggie stands before a counter, sleepwalking through another day, living that half-existence of work. The cash register rings anachronistically, as she counts out the change of yet another boring sale. The woman standing across from her is aging quickly, purchasing hip new clothes to fight back the wrinkles. The young woman watches the aging one walking languidly towards the door, as if walking were below her lofty station. As the be-postered door shuts her off from the remainder of Maggie's life.

Maggie slumps with practiced weight onto her little stool. She softly fingers the ancient keys of the register and imagines a line of cars on the way to a funeral or a wedding. She looks at the floors, in no need of cleaning. She looks to the shelves of “antiques” and kitsch items, in no need of arranging. She stares back at the floor and wonders if tonight will be the night to reunite with John.

The door opens again, interrupting her naval gazing session, revealing a tall, fat man in fashionable, but outdated clothing. Her attention perks up at the entry of this giant. As she stands to greet her friend, an unknown face with an unfamiliar mustache looks back at her. Just another hipster, she thinks, far past his irony expiration date. Hephaestus would wear that suit well, she imagines, as the stranger approaches. She mimes interest as he asks about items and the date and weight of various things. She goes through the motions, by rote, until he, and the day, are gone. The lights are shut off, as she shuts off the day, forever relegated to the past with the simple locking of a door.

It will not be tonight, she thinks. I am too tired, too bored to allow him back in. I'll visit after work tomorrow, or maybe

Thursday, or if things go poorly, this weekend. Her internal time-line stretches forward as her legs move at pace. From the corner of her eye she spots, sitting in a gutter, a small plastic dinosaur. It's orange skin sits in contrast to the disintegrating leaves. She continues her walk holding the vision of that discolored children's toy, reminiscing on a man who once saw such things with such different eyes.

The faintest hint of breath can be seen on the air before her lips as she dreams of a world full of better times and more interesting company. The night gathers up shards of frost, tossing them upon the trees and fallen leaves which mark her walk home.

## 38. The Hermit.

The sun is sitting, static, and the birds are watching with disinterest as a man called John is walking the middle of a rarely used dirt road.

The sun is stalled in its progress and he is again walking towards nothing in particular.

The sun is arrested in the sky and the office is growing smaller behind him.

His vision is set in the style of his youth. He watches the birds and trees sitting in the warmth and comfort of another day left to their own designs. The trees, the birds, the animals of various transparencies, all agree to hold onto this day, to grasp the last autumnal rays of warmth, storing energy for the coming winter.

He is gaining speed towards the small shop where he can find Maggie. He hopes that the brightness of the day, and the brightness of his mood, will sway her into conversation about their recent pasts. The town is now coming into view and into view again with the eyes of the peripheral.

He is distracted, suddenly, by an eddy of energy to his left. An old mansion dotted with doors, seemingly without use, grabs John's attention. He recalls references to this place in the confused and obfuscated words of Hephaestus: The Place of Doors and Vortices. Until then he had assumed it to be located elsewhere, in some far off realm away from both hill and Tree.

He feels kinship to this place, of recognition through unfamiliarity, like the houses in your dreams, so familiar yet so unknown.

He approaches cautiously, crossing the rarely traveled street, feeling no fear or hesitation as in the basement or on the hill.

John approaches the house, its face bisected by a corridor filled with shadow. The backyard can be faintly seen in the distance. He enters the bisection, a hallway of Victorian doors of purple and green. 'Of course it would be a hall of doors', he thinks. 'What else would I find by following the path of Hephaestus.'

He looks to find which would be proper to knock upon, and spots a lone rope swinging from a windowsill. He has learned much in the weeks since his life split from normalcy of youth to the vision of the younger. John decides to pull the chord. He dodges falling masonry and stumbles into the railing behind him, falling through a now open door.

From the now open door a wave of musty air assaults John. A moving set of moth eaten clothes, filled with a bent-over, wrinkled person, approaches John from within.

“You must be the new one. Bonobus has told me of you. I expect you will fix the damage you have wrought to my home in good speed, or expect a visit in the night. I am Gideon. Please be at peace here.”

The elderly man, smiling at John sitting on the ground, motions to a room of couches. It is a mirror of a section of the office in the woods, though coated in dust and tinted with the strain of age. He sees that John recognizes the seats, finding humor in his confusion.

“Hi. Sorry, I, uh, I didn't mean to break anything. I thought the rope was a bell.”

“Don't think that just because it happens at your silly place on the hill, it will happen everywhere. This locality is an independent thinking satellite. Our voices are reserved for ritual and song.”

“I am not from the place on the hill. No one is, anymore. I am from the office in the woods."

"Fine, fine, woodsman, I see your point. Now give me your name so we may continue our discourse."

"I'm John… the Younger."

"I am Gideon the Rested. You are John the Watcher as long as you sit under these roofs. Do not insult an old man with familiar names and poor introductions. And say hello to the couch. It knows you, does it not?"

"Yes, well, we have one much like it at the office. Hello couch. Hello seats. Hello, Gideon the Rested. What place is this? It reminds me of the office."

John fails to notice that he now thinks of the office in the woods as home.

"Perceptive boy, he's right to trust you. This is a place stuck between. We are a place of doors and patient waiting. We hold allegiance to the place on the hill and the office in the woods. We hunt no quarry here though. So please no attacks on innocent things whilst in my vicinity."

John believes he has found a man who can be trusted to explain Hephaestus's cryptic leavings. Gideon believes he is speaking to John's name giver. Gideon chose a path through the doors in the woods, and the places in the hills, which left him without tree or memory of such things as death or transformation of states.

"The place on the hill is wasted. I am to take it back."

"Wasted? It is perfect and new. I saw it myself not but yesterday. Moreover, take it? Just walk in and rule? That is exactly the way you and that young thing have always done it, since the start. And tell that Hephaestus that if I am to entertain his compatriots he better present them in person."

"Which young thing? The Keeper of our Tree?"

“No, not him. He is ancient. I am speaking of our youthful master, Mr. Hephaestus James Bonobus himself. You and he are bound for trouble. Two places so close will cause problems. The animals will be drawn there. You, John, the Watcher of the keep, must keep that brazen oaf in check before he gets hurt.”

John, as Gideon speaks, looks to the walls of the place of doors, covered in sepia newsprint and ancient pictures. In the dusty frames he can see youthful photos of Hephaestus, Dura, Gideon, Maggie, himself, his brother, Cassiel, and various others of familiar visage and forgotten names. John sees within these frames the final memory of the generation before his, the dead and dying frozen in lifeless youth.

He knows that Gideon has not moved on. He knows that Gideon does not recognize the turning of the cycle. The notions of Gideon are years out of date and skewed to an unfamiliar perspective.

“Gideon, the Rested, how is it that you know Hephaestus so well?”

“I helped him build that place in the woods while you were out gallivanting in the other place. Your Tree wept night and day; no treats or rituals could calm it. I know him because I was once like you two, young and needing of great things. When you enter The Tree you will understand young master.”

“And, I, you know as John… The Watcher?”

“Yes, yes, that little ball of confusion has called you that for years, ever since you were called to him and him to you. My wife and I were watchers while that place was built. He told us of his other self, traveling in the foreign realms… John the Watcher, the bringer of things, the bold man who can enter into their place and run without incident… always John the Watcher. Until such a day that another is necessary, then John the Elder, but no sooner than the time of picking a Younger. You know this. That, I am sure of.”

“I am sorry, Gideon the Rested. I was confused for a moment.

I am, of course, John the Watcher, trusted compatriot of Hephaestus, gone these long years in campaign to the other place. You know, memory is a funny thing sometimes."

John mimics the language of the office, and the books. He knows this Gideon believes him to be his predecessor. He looks more carefully and sees this place as more reflection than substance, a shadow of the office, a faded picture of something long past yet stubbornly remaining.

"Of course, of course, we all fall into ourselves at times. Care for tea, or water, or some such thing which one offers?"

"No, thank you, I have eaten and drank. How do you like the place on the hill? Do you think the work that goes on there will be good?"

"It will be good as long as you tread carefully around the land inside the land. That place holds its allegiance to the pure and old, not our kin. It will be good if you take the place slowly. If you battle with pure vision, and respect the fact that they can win as easily as you can, then, yes, I think the work will be good, and the Trees will grow with astounding speed. Blessed be those that grow for us."

"Yes, blessed be the Trees in the woods and newly on the hill."

John has a feeling it is time to leave. This man is old and confused. His vision is broken and stuck somewhere before John's arrival.

"Gideon, the Rested, I must be going. Thank you for your kind hospitality. Please know that I will have your sill repaired in the coming days. Good day."

"Good day to you, John the Watcher. Be careful upon your hill, and more so below it. There is no greater sadness then when a tree is felled by those things. Do not let it happen."

John looks back as he walks away from the building of doors

to confirm his suspicions of what had happened there. No tree stands in the yard, simply two mounds of disrupted dirt. His office, his purpose, both felled in some distant past. John sees that this man is adrift with no reason, no vocation to show him the way.

He walks, again, towards the town, unsure of his original reason for going. He is starting to realize that time and reason are, in fact, funny things sometimes.

In a place of too many doors, a man sits as statuary. In a place of doors, a man pictures entrances to lost places, exits into a world that made sense. In a place of doors, a man is moving towards his end, full of regret and the lamentations of a life spent alone.

## 39. Justice (inverted).

An unexpected knock at the door of the offices of HJ Bonobus is a rare thing. The rapping echoes through the walls, and into the darker places beneath. John, roused from his study of the scant papers of the fallen saint of that place, rises from the couch, taking special precaution not to disturb the plate next to him. He approaches the sound of the knocking, unsure as to its origin. Somewhere from within him, a memory stirs of sirens and handcuffs, of loud knocking and elaborate tales. Opening the door he is startled to see a man in his thirties dressed in a police costume.

"Hello Mister Constable."

"Hello Sir, I'm Detective Robert Wilson," he takes out a small notebook as he pronounces the word Detective like the impact of a blunt object. "Is this the HJ Bone-e-bus Company?"

"Yes, it is. What, may I ask, brings you to our esteemed locality?"

"We'll get to that. Are you, John? You're acquainted with one Cassiel Landry?"

"Yes. I know Cass from the sundries store. I am unsure of his last name. And I am John."

"Last name, John?"

"What is this all about? Cass in some trouble?"

"Mr. Landry has gone missing, sir. Judging from the state of his store, we have suspicions of foul play. We're simply here to investigate all possibilities."

"Indeed. Possibilities everywhere, all to be explored, the cornerstone of this very business. I have not seen Cass in months. I heard the shop closed, but it has been a rent check away from that the entire time I have known him. You're saying he's gone?"

"Yes, sir. When was the last time you saw him? Do you know the date exactly?"

"It was May the 5th. I was to borrow from him a certain item. It became an unnecessary barter, for his knowledge served more as a unit of exchange than a physical object."

"Sir, this is serious."

"I am completely serious, Detective. I speak with the clarity that I should assume all people in league with an authority should posses."

"What is your last name, John?"

"That is my business and my business alone. I am sorry, but I keep certain aspects of myself private. Call me John the Younger if you wish."

"Tell me your last name, sir."

"Am I under investigation? If you have no warrant or reason for your uninvited visit, I should very much like this conversation to end. You disturb our business with your negative energy and improper speech."

"So you refuse to give me your name? May I come in and take a look around?"

"You may not."

His hand feverishly scrawling notes, "Why is that, exactly?"

"Because this is a place of sensitive items and business. So unless you show me the proper respect and documentation you may not enter this sacred spot."

"Okay, John…" he looks to his pad, "the Younger. Expect me back with warrant in hand. And don't think I didn't look up your file before I stopped by for this little visit. Dark things John, dark things."

He glares at the blue suited man, "You insult him by bringing up that memory. Good day 'sir', though I sully the term with such unpropitious usage."

"Fine, be aggressive. I will be back, John. This will not end well for you."

With that the door is slammed, and the house moves slightly. The couch is fuming, the greenhouse in a froth. John's anger is complete, all encompassing. The house is waiting for fury, battening itself down for the torrential rage. His breath is staggered, his vision red with discord. The birds outside flee in terror.

"He will not insult this place again. This I swear on the names of the previous. He will fall to ruin before he insults me again."

Then, as quickly as it rose, the wave of anger falls back. He is again calm.

He lets go.

The walls expand in relief; the glass clears; the scales balance.

Kali, eyes planted firmly upon the floor, enters sheepishly into the room.

"Oh dear… John, that was quite a show. Not since the days of the fall has such anger been felt. It is good you learned to let go so quickly. Most of us take years of meditative perception to control those deeper emotions."

"That thing in the suit insulted the memory of someone long since gone. I do not take kindly to the ones who disturb the rest of those who deserve rest. He brings news of missing friends; he threatens dead relatives. He oversteps what little welcome he was given."

"Oh John, your fury is just, your control is subtle and precise. Be glad now that you have shown the patience of someone in your esteemed position," she places her hand, tiny and warm, on his cheek. "You have done well this day."

"Thank you, Kali of the desk. Please, if you could look at me, I could become whole again."

Her gaze on his, her hand on his; the graves stay full; the blood stays hidden away. In the night, they become as one being; in the night another circle is completed.

## 40. Ascensions and root cellars.

In the morning, the familiar waves of uncertainty wash upon John. He wakens to the movement of the bed, the writhing in the walls. He exists now, as he will in later days, in a large room diagonal to the greenhouse, mercy seat to the heart of the periphery.

Kali lays on the couch in the corner.

The Child stands in the yard.

And somewhere on the upper floors walks the wrinkled visage of Dura.

The building hums with the sounds of new management.

The whispers from the lower parts grow quieter with the promises of expulsion. The energy from the hill is beginning to flow downward, probing at the woods, probing at annexation.

John feels the movements from higher to low, and in his dreams he knows the truth of the Trees. In his dreams he sits, older, and less himself, on the lawn, on the mountain.

Beneath the grass the denizens of a once pure world knock and howl. He knows the Elder as he breathes softly. The Elder knows the Younger as the sight becomes precise. The calling of the hill is truth, and the wisdom of Hephaestus will come to pass.

He awakes to filtered sunlight and fluttering birds of arguable existence. He looks to Kali sleeping on the couch, an oversized coat as her blanket. He finds himself tempted to wake her, to reunite after hours spent away in unconsciousness. He looks out the window to see The Child standing, balloons at the ready. John has acclimated to this place, but not its entirety. He feels the polar shifts and tidal forces of the periphery as he passes from room to room.

He decides the time to explore is long since due, and the start would be the foggy place of battle Hephaestus showed him, on the day of his ascension. After ten minutes of attempting to recreate a walk from the parlor to the room of his battle he is flustered, the house in constant movement disrupting his navigation.

“I have to be close,” he mutters to himself. “We followed the wall with the painting, down the steps and there it was. I need to think more like him. I need to stop fighting his influence. If I think like Hephaestus, maybe I can function like him.”

He puffs out his chest and inhales. He sweeps his hand in a grand gesture, imagining his carriage being double its size. His hand, upon completion of his giant's movement hits, a little too hard, a doorknob.

“Of course…”

He whispers curses as he sees the top of a flight of stairs. Upon the wall above the top-most step is an art-deco painting of Jesus. Its eyes follow John's descent.

## 41. The High Priestess of quantum entanglement.

"Where…? It was here. Right here. There's the chair he sat in and laughed. Hi chair! Where the hell is the door?"

John is stammering to himself after an hour of fruitless searching. He has found the place he was looking for. Though it has dawned on him that he may lack the perception to gain entry. He sweeps his hands widely. He makes speeches about nothing in a bold voice. He imagines himself dressed as Sherlock Holmes. He slips his back down the wall and sits heavy, despondent.

So enters Kali of the desk to light the way.

"Mr. The Younger, I thought you may have come down here. How goes your sitting on the floor?"

"Kali! Where is the room with the flower door and old furniture? I swear it was right here."

"Oh, loveliest John! You could not be more wrong this day! How silly to find that door where last you looked. I assumed that you would have learned the ways of this place by now."

"What do you mean? It was right here."

"It was there because Bonobus wanted it there. He was the master of this place, as you are the place on the hill. Since you are technically him, for the moment, you may make doors as you wish. Be careful of this though. It can become addictive after a fashion. You will find yourself with more doors than places in need of going. You become detached and obsessed with the trivial things, like cleanly porches and barren lawns."

"Gideon."

"Indeed. You are the first to find him in many years. I am pleased he still draws breath, though not in the way we would wish. A man without a Tree is no man at all. Sometimes it is that way for the later years of a couples' life. He and his other will find peace and new dirt soon enough, and we will be them in the eventuality. Now, let us find your door."

So it appears, as real and apparent as on the day he last walked through it. John looks with both sights and it appears the same. The office has a way of bonding the two together, the old and the new, the created and the perceived, the invented and the solid. The office, to John and to the others of his sight, is used as a nexus, a place of overlap between one perception and the other.

"There you go young master. Enter as you wish."

"How did you do that? Or did we? How?"

"Well, look closer. I believe your initial tour was too short for your later good. I recommend exploring this place further before you reclaim the place of dead things. Remember my love, there is no sight, only the perception. Thinking linearly will be your end, as it was before."

She quiets him with a look, and holds his hand. They walk into the room of the broken chair and the memory of battle. The room exhales upon their entry. The room is expecting the worst for the coming days. The room is close to something deeper still. John and Kali walk into the recesses, from the darkness appears two doors.

"You take the right and I the left, for fear we will not meet on the other side."

"Oh John, you do learn some things quickly. But let us both walk right, just this one time, and see the place which gives so much anxiety to our shared beloved."

They enter the door to the right. The world shatters. The light appears poorly diffused as they exit from a storm cellar to a sunny patch of grass in the middle of a grove of trees, blackened from recent fires.

Kali falls to her knees, grasping desperately at John's leg. John grabs back in horror. He feels the rot and slaughter of this place. He spies the top of a building slightly higher up through the charcoal drawings of trees. He knows this is the hill, the place of dead things. He knows now that Kali's tree was among the charcoal. He knows that he lays dead, still, in the land below the land. John and Kali stand in the grove of dead trees, in the path of the office on the hill, in the land of dead things. John and Kali stand in the wake of an all-consuming echo.

“I only show you this now so you may know what has been seen and what needs to be made whole again. This place was once green and alive. A child held balloons, your child. The Trees sang with blessed merriment. Now, it is burnt. Now it is dead, an ossuary of trees as reminder of the sins of our shared past. The people who ran this place believed in too many gods, too many variations upon the periphery. I bring you here because this place is part of you still, and you will repeat the same mistakes. We of the woods trust in you, John the Younger, to right what you have broken. We of the woods believe you will set this place right.”

He begins to realize his place in this dance; or, his place as it would appear to an observer from outside this place, if one such as that could exist. The placing of eyes upon his narrative would shift the perspective, allowing in too much of the world as it was, the world as fixed by a metaphorical brain stem in a yard, and a basement of broken debris from a violence subsumed by story and delusion.

"I, he… we did this, didn't we? When I was the older and the younger me, the one who speaks still, was not yet broken: I spoke ruin to this place."

"We all hold sins from the previous turns. When I was her, who now waits above, I would have acted as your mother, coddling you too often, and without sight. When I was her, I let this happen for my love of him that is you. We all hold sins from the previous turns. All we can do is try to clean up the bloodied mess of lives left to selfish insanities and greedy illusions."

He sees Kali as the camera, the universe as uncaring and ineffective. He feels the weight of guilt, of murder, the karma as understood within a grove of broken and burnt trees.

"How do I fix it?"

"You become what you once were. You will bring back the elder name and invoke it upon these dead things. You will stride with a fury and a depth of field yet unknown into the land beneath this land, and reign. You will plant new trees to make up for your mistakes. You fix it by not letting yourself become distracted. You will see. He has faith in you, as do I. We will christen this place in the blood of what has no place. We will destroy him as he destroyed this once perfect haven of those with the sight."

They sit, cross-legged and staring at the tattered remains of something once pure. The business of the day is done, and they sit like stone Buddhas waiting for the coming of night.

The wails and pops from the earth are like rain on the still glowing embers of something long ago burnt.

They sit with hands held, and eyes watering.

They sit until the pain is distributed evenly, until he knows the exposed nerve that is Kali.

They sit until the torment of her days after the fall and her failure to keep the old guard in line become as much a part of him as of her.

They sit until he understands the drain of her accord with the place in the woods.

As the night comes, with chaotic stars and ill omens, she beckons him to leave. As the night comes, a door in the grass opens to the pouring of the light. Holding hands, they descend the stairs, the storm doors closing them off from the vision of destruction they had lived in for those hours. John and Kali leave that place to the dark that so perfectly mirrors the history as perceived by a broken camera.

He is the first to speak in the darkened room of dust and broken things, "I'm so sorry. If he only knew, what it would become… I'm sorry."

"Peace. You have been forgiven of that since the day you walked back through our doors. Now, let us find music and nourishment, the work will be long tomorrow."

So it is that they retire into the upper reaches of the house, to sit and listen to the scratches and pops of Bonobus' record player. And so the house receives them, shutting the door in the basement permanently: a wound poorly sutured, a neuron cauterized.

The place on the hill sits in wait for the coming battle. The thing on the hill sits in fear of the newest to the sight. The two places sit, and accept the completeness that is the swallowing night.

And so, under the hill, the elder whispers, and the periphery wavers in its consistency.

John the Elder has held his name for too long.

The office in the woods sits in silent mourning for the dying generation.

# 42. The past.

**The past:** Made up by a series of conversations and narratives taking place in a strange office in an odd set of woods, as bisected by alternate realities full of lost civilizations and a mystic order of powerful seers. Those conversations were had by the following:

**John**: The Younger; the elder; the newest edition to this world; one of its oldest denizens is a man whose vision is wildly strong and terribly, profoundly broken. He is the route of all resistance; he is the aether through which all narratives must flow. He walks in broken trees as symbols.

**Kali**: The documentarian of past things. Kali has danced in various bodies, in various times. Kali is the only one with a sense of compassion towards this cyclical farce. She says that John was once a man who became a monster, who cut down trees and screamed with bloodied throat into the universe a hate-filled message. Kali says that John is reborn again, as John the Younger, to make right his sinful and bloody past.

**Dura and Gideon**: They are but tertiary things, barely visible in the gloaming of the times John lives through. One lives out his days as a failed seer. The other is to die a worker's death. They stink of rot, of aging. They will soon, if all is to be believed, leave this place violently.

**Maggie**: She sits in her apartment, waiting to be let back into John's world. She will regret this in the future, if a future is something we can predict. She will regret this if the coming actions can be documented by their actors.

**The Child in the yard**: The caretaker of the brain stem… the monster in the grass… The Tree. In a blessed synchronicity he is interchangeable with his charge. He is a thing of immensity, of boundless sight and preternatural grace. He is cared for, in perpetuity, by a group of thinkers gathered in a house.

**The Police:** A group of uniforms filled with people who often get confused by groups of people gathered together in the woods. The elder statesmen of this clandestine cabal gives nods and respect to the people of the woods.

**Hephaestus James Bonobus**: Hephaestus was a profoundly fat man who told lies and deceits. He was beloved despite or because of their telling. He was a father, a brother, and the tutor of the newcomers' nascent philosophy. He, if all were perfect, would have been a hero in a story. But the world of the periphery is not perfect, as long as the camera remains broken, as long as the mere observation changes the results.

**The Tree**: Oh god, The Tree. It is the root, the base of all that happens around it. It is, at its core, a metaphor for self, a metaphor for brain stems and pineal glands. It eats balloons and sprays rebirth upon the soil. The Tree could be the camera, if the camera could exist.

## 43. Visitation Rites.

It is morning, and the yard is calm with The Child's caretaking.

The office breathes with the ease of sleep.

Dura exists like a whisper in the upper reaches, while Kali paces the lower floors in hope of epiphany.

John sips coffee at a table alone. He thinks of the weeks passed in a perfect fog. He wonders what happened to his old apartment, his belongings, his old life. He wonders how he will approach the place on the hill. He thinks of Kali, and of Maggie. He misses them both, though one still wanders through his daily existence.

He idly changes from one sight to the other, sending out heart-like pulses into the periphery.

He is a beacon in the woods.

The others of the office feel his torpor and recognize it as the vestments of Hephaestus.

They wait for his signal to return to a semblance of routine.

The doorbell rings.

The house stirs awake. The house buzzes with the unexpected.

The house is rarely surprised. When a surprise happens, it is treated with grandiosity and joy. Today it is joyous with the prospect of the unknown.

Kali looks to the ceiling, knowing she cannot be part of the coming meeting.

The creature of the upper reaches shimmers in consistency, knowing her time is near.

The Child wanders in the yard.

John answers the door, and through both sets of eyes, he is shocked. What is shown to him upon his doorstep is the glowing vision of Maggie, a loss of words and a glimmer of what is to come.

“I met him.”

“Bonobus… I should have assumed as much. Please enter and be welcomed. You are a joy to this place, Maggie of the old apartment.”

He bows with a half joking flourish and begs her entry.

“Thank you. So this is what had devoured you the past two months. It's nicer than I'd imagined. Hello couch!” John flashes a look of befuddlement and shock at her greeting.

“The fat man said you'd get a kick out of that. I have no idea why.”

“I say that often, lately. How are you?”

“Fine, I guess. Did I tell you I moved?”

"I heard you took Cassiel's place after he took off. How is it?"

"It's weird knowing that you knew him, but it's nice overall. On to you, what, if I may ask, are you doing here, exactly?”

“Well, that's a long story, and one I'm not all together sure I know the details of. But, if you'd let me, I'd like to try and tell you.”

“I'd love to. Though try to keep the weirdness to a minimum.

Your boss has a way of speaking that makes me think this isn't such a bad place. Where is he today? I'd like to thank him for the tea."

"Ah, well, he's in the yard… after a fashion. Let us get some cookies and I'll introduce you to The Child and The Tree. I have a feeling this will take awhile."

So they walk through the office in the woods. The mood shifts from empty to anticipatory. Kali stalks in the basement like a wounded pet. The Child in the yard shivers. The bodies of what came before lay motionless, rotting.

## 44. The Lovers (reversed).

They stand in the waiting room, Maggie shifting her weight from right foot to left. John is finished with his tale of the days since their last meeting. She is frightened and nervous. He is proud of his moments of eloquence.

"John. I will refrain from running from this place for the moment. But, I must say, your story is an odd one. You can't actually expect me to believe in floating animals and fights in basements with no proof. Show me something. I've got my mind and my eyes wide open. Prove to me that I'm not nuts for coming here."

"I would love to prove to you the truth of this place. Let's start with the bathroom!"

He speaks with exuberance, mimicking as best he can the boom and vigor of Bonobus on his first walk through the stranger lands of his current life.

"Why?"

"Well, it's... I don't know. It's not actually a bathroom at all, but some kind of greenhouse of fish and plants... let me show you, it will be easier."

She sighs heavily, "Okay. But make it quick, this place is starting to creep me out."

"It did the same thing to me. But believe me that I think of it as home now. Ah, here it is, the door marked W.C... Shoes must be removed before entering this sacred spot. Please, no argument from the visitors. Rules are made so they may fit their name."

"Christ, John, there's like an inch of dirty water on the floor. I'm not going in there with hip waders on, let alone my bare feet."

"No, it's not fetid."

He lifts up his foot to remove his shoe.

"It's really like an aquarium for strange periphery animals."

He stands with bare feet.

"Maggie, believe me, it's magical."

"John… I'm not going into a bathroom half full of nasty water with no shoes on, it's seriously gross and frankly unhealthy. You probably have black mold all over this place."

He grabs her arm, "No, okay, leave on your shoes but let me show you the plants in the urinal."

She shirks her arm back from his grasp, "John, what the hell? Listen to yourself. You want me, on the first day seeing you in months, to walk into piss water to look at plants in a urinal. Can you not see how nutty this all is?"

"Yeah, okay, fine, let us skip this part. Maybe something easier to take in would make you more comfortable with all this. Let's show you Dura and the kaleidoscopic eye in the brass machine."

"The what?"

"The old camera which removed my glasses. Believe I spoke of it to you on my first day."

"No, let's not. I don't think an old camera will prove anything. Let me see The Tree John… let me see The Tree."

"Oh, Maggie my loveliest! What a great idea! Let us visit The Child in the yard and his charge The Tree!"

They exit through cellar door. The boy half-smiles at Maggie's approach. Maggie looks to The Tree, and to The Child's clutch of balloons. She knows these things from John's telling. The balloons seem animal to her; the boy unsettling; the grass verdant; The Tree, slightly swaying in a nonexistent breeze.

"Oh god, John. It's... it's... wrong." Maggie says pointing at The Child, "What is that thing?"

Sometimes a light is best left off. Sometimes a balloon must remain a balloon.

"That's The Child in the yard, Keeper of The Tree. Keeper, this is Maggie. Maggie this is The Child in the yard."

He recoils from her, and her him. They speak in unison:

"NO."

The boy turns his back to them, stroking one balloon after the other, calming them. In the periphery, the animals scream on their strings. In the periphery, the boy who is a man can barely hold back their flight. John looks in wonder at this loss of control. Maggie was hurting them, and disturbing The Child.

"John. Let's go back in. I don't like it out here. The tree... the child... everything is wrong."

She tries to point to The Tree; he grabs her hand before reaching parallel, as understood by maths unrelated.

"Please, do not point, company policy. We will return inside."

Maggie turns in retreat and he follows. Inside, they find a comfortable spot and John begins to soothe the chaos this artificial tour has caused in her. John focusing with the old sight, ignoring the screams of the yard and of the basement, begins to talk her back into a perception of reality she can hold onto.

In a comfortable chair across from an indiscreet couch, they create a story for the months in which they were apart. He knows

Maggie has some influence here. He knows that he will have to figure out why it is that she can make the balloons scream and the child rudely turn.

Maggie sits uncomfortable, feeling like the air was foul or the ghosts were unsettled.

The house groans in uncomfortable movement.

Maggie says that it is time to leave, and John retorts with confusing words.

Maggie stands, and with worried eyes wishes him farewell. As John looks over her head with lifeless eyes.

The door closes shut, and he stands with doll's eyes, beginning to mutter mantras into the void.

In the basement, Kali wails against the intrusion: gnashing teeth and kicking walls.

It is a day worthy of names, though no chronicler exists to witness.

## 45. Generations.

In the gathering dark, the child in the yard walks in slow circles as Kali and John approach from the storm cellar.

"You look older today Keeper of The Tree. It suits you."

"The Tree is sated, and such is my growth. Soon I will return to the house. The new trees will have their start soon, I believe. The last pair is fading even as we speak."

Kali grabs the child's arm, "He does not know these things yet. Let it come in the time in which she arrives and we become again."

"Of course. John of the hill, please excuse my indiscretion. If you do not mind, I shall take the room on the third floor as my own."

"It's yours."

The three enter the office.

The office is sated.

The ghosts on the hill wail as the things which bear no name writhe and stumble in the more indistinguishable places. The time of movement is upon this place: the pairings are strong; the Trees demand the old guard to give way to the shoots of new growth.

The child moves himself into the upper floors. Kali leaves to the lower while John sleeps in the bed of a fallen king, dark and warm. This sleep will be the last of the old ways.

In the darkness, the holder of old names rises, and in the darkness he comes to Gideon, Keeper of doors.

His blood is spilled upon the floor, and the Trees of the woods scream for their loss.

A blade repeatedly glistens in the sepia light of a house with too many doors. That same sepia light lays upon the carpet, which lays under Gideon: stopped, bloodied. A shadow in the shape of a person drinks heavily from him, feeding the hill, defining his name.

He is the Keeper of names, the betrayer of the hill, the destroyer of the old ways. He will enter the office when the other of the pair falls in the woods. His footfalls are soft, as the stain on the carpet spreads towards the door, now shutting behind soft footfalls.

John wakes with a start.

A pained scream sends screeching alarms from his deepest recesses as he throws off his bedding and sprints to The Tree.

In the yard the three stand once again, child, Kali and John stand with tears universally streaming.

The child falls to the ground and pulls at his hair.

The Tree knows that the old ways are nearing an end unless new ground is fertilized, and fertilized soon.

In the house, a violent mass has stood over Dura, now cold and stilled.

The three in the yard look up and see the shadow.

The three in the yard are stopped by the wail of the denizens of the other side.

The three in the yard look to the periphery and the yard sways back with the squirming shadows of the lower kinds.

The remains of a person thrown from the upper reaches of the house sail through the air, silently. With the sound of cracking bones and breaking branches, it bounces upon impact with the grass. A desiccated shape lays, still, upon the grass. Its empty sockets staring without sight at a rusting heap covered in plants.

In the grass, two empty shells exist in silent memory of a time when faded pictures on ancient walls were yet young, documentation not yet made memory.

The child and Kali speak in unison, the song of the name;

"He is here. The Elder has come to claim the remaining elders."

The Trees stop their swaying and so settle to eventual death.

The shadow form of a man slowly seeps its way from the upper window to the grass.

Wavering, transparent.

A voice from nowhere is heard by John and the others.

"The old ways are done. You have been reborn from the fruit as destroyer of this place, as once I was destroyer. The child and the girl will follow, as well the one you are keeping off campus. You should not have made it this far, John. I shall await your arrival upon the hill."

With that utterance, the shadow fractures into wisps of smoke, carried on the autumnal breeze into the woods surrounding the office.

"That was me, wasn't it?"

John feels, upon the utterance of his statement, that his world will be forever changed. He sees the darker part of the periphery, and it looks back with familiar eyes.

Kali inches closer to him, a small, polite comfort in the dark, "Yes, beloved, in a way that is you. But be at peace, it is not you fully. It is a manifestation of your past. A specific darkness you have held onto has allowed it to take form again. That thing from the hill is what once was called John the Elder, which was once paired with Hephaestus. He holds his name too long. He perverts the hill and feeds from the Trees. You will not be him unless you fail on the hill, then all will be lost."

John, lost in the idea of simultaneous life and death stammers, "But, I thought he was dead."

"He is. The waif will explain it to you in time," The Child speaks as law. There is no vacillation or argument to be found in his preternatural gravel. "Now, let us find what is left of Dura and give to The Tree what may be left. I will send Kali to Gideon. I believe he has been felled as well. You will contact your Maggie and under auspice of night enter into the place of doors. It will need a caretaker, and if she can find it, as we know she can, it is hers. John the Younger, Keeper of the hill, manager *in nominus*, you must make sure to not allow her and the waif to share a space quite yet. It is something you must see to understand, and that sight cannot come until the preparations for the hill are complete. John, it is your duty to save us from the mistakes of our predecessors."

"I will take her there, and she will sit in wait for the arrival of their meeting. I cannot claim to know your logic, but I trust you, my friend Keeper. Your tree will be safe, and that hill will again flourish. The HJ Bonobus Corp will thrive in waiting for the return of its lost master. When I see the fat man again, he will be pleased at what we've done here."

The child looks to the man, and the man sees the child shift in consistency once again. The child will soon be adult, fully vested in this place. A new Keeper will be found and he will grow after The Tree is sated. The circles and vortices will tighten and the periphery will move closer to this place, the shadows will abate and the walls will grow green with the energies of the newly sighted.

## 46. The Woodsman and the Elder reminiscing.

"I recall our time in the desert," The Woodsman spoke with whispered reverence. "I recall our stomachs growling after days of nothing but water, and the dried sacraments from those early trees."

"A fine thing to recall," The Elder smiled and looked into the distance. "I recall the time before that, when we had those older names which would tangle our tongues as the rituals progressed."

"Ah, yes, a grand memory to hold my dearest friend. At times I can almost see our old faces. At times I still taste the earliest fruits, and smell those ancient places."

It was a time when two old men, in the bodies of those yet young, told tales of days long gone.

It was a time when two followers of tangential paths spoke with wisdom and invented myths.

It was a time, now long gone, that a man with a forgotten name spoke to a man with a name so old it no longer held meaning in the mouths of the modern.

It was a time where two men, Woodsman and Elder, glowed with love and familiarity with the other. They spoke with truth. They hunted with precision. They ate the fruit of the newly grown trees. They fasted in the desert. They feasted in the woods.

It was a time, now long gone, in which invention was indistinct from memory. Two men had yet to make the mistakes which would define their later lifetimes.

## 47. The Towers rebuilt from memory.

John stands at the door to Maggie's apartment holding a flower folded from leaves, the child's doing. He looks into the nature of the door and sees the familiar writhing lines and transparent filaments, the markers of the periphery.

John is suspecting that Maggie's role in the worlds of the periphery is something deeper than he knows. It is something beyond the bounds of safety from the seething masses of the hill and the other place. He knows she must take leave to the land on which Gideon lost his tree. He believes that this meeting will mark her entry into his world. This visit will offer her the position of Keeper in the place of doors. She will be safe in a place of her own power, her auspice.

The door is opened.

Maggie's face alights.

John grins stupidly.

He locks her eyes to his own as he grandiosely hands her the green rose. She smells it, laughing lightly.

“Thank you for coming. And for the wonderful rose. Care to come in?”

The apartment is full of shadows and the tricks of light, which bespeak the perversion of the purer land. John feels a panic hoping he will not have to battle some menacing thing. He fears Maggie will run from him forever.

"Thanks. We've much to discuss."

“I have to tell you. I only got in contact because my reaction to that place didn't make sense. And, well, I figured that if I'm getting thrown off by a place that means there is probably something to that place, that feeling. Does that make sense?”

“Of course… of course. While one side is patient the other is frantic. Of course, of course, the place would vibrate with you strangely. I will endeavor to fix that… I will make sure you are comfortable.”

“John, are you alright? You seem jumpy. What happened to that Zen master vibe you had than last we spoke?”

“I'm fine, just fine, but your new place, it… it has something about it that unsettles me."

"It’s got to be weird, being here without Cassiel."

"I can't remember the last time. Cass and I were having beers, listening to one of his obscure, joyless, yet oddly interesting records. I can't believe he'd just up and leave without telling anyone…”

"John… he probably…"

He interrupts, "Now, though, it feels off, like we're being watched.”

Little does he know that he is watched at all times when outside the office, the watchers of the hill swift and cunning.

“Yeah. It is a little creepy… I think. But it's home for the moment. You did hear about what happened? Right?"

"Yes. I received word."

"You… received word? That's it?"

"Yes. I have hope for his swift return."

She sighs heavily, gathering herself, regaining calm.

"So, what brings you?"

"It's about the office. I know you felt something when you were there," she nods in tacit agreement. "Well, it's complicated, more so than I can explain right now. But I have to show you something… somewhere, I mean. You aren't safe right now."

"Why am I unsafe?"

She sounds unconvinced of her question. Since her visit with Hephaestus she has felt unease around her. A general, nameless, malaise has set upon her. It is as if she was playacting life, not actually participating in the act of living.

"The one who had my name previous to me, I believe he sees something in you that we are supposed to use. He has ended the last two of the previous ones, Dura and Gideon. We need you to be our new Gideon. You will take over the place of doors and make it right again. Or, maybe wait there until we conquer the hill. It is very unclear. But you must find the place of doors, that much is known."

She smiles broadly at him. He is surprised at her reaction, expecting an argument and his dismissal from the premises. Reaching across the table, she holds his hand, "John, I haven't a single clue as to what you just said. But I know that you believe it. So, if it means we have to take a little walk to find some doors to get you back in my life, so be it. But let's be clear here, you are doing this for what you believe are good purposes?"

And with that, John feels the stirring of the new coupling, the lurching energies of a new generation forming. He speaks with an authority he knows only from the tone of his once great master, "I know what we do is for the only good purpose. We will show the world what it once was, and will be again. We will no longer be confined to the periphery."

"Sure. That sounds fine; I guess. Do all of you talk like that?"

"Oh, yeah, I suppose histrionics sort of comes with the office. You will see, hopefully."

And so they embrace and prepare for the journey to her new home. So it is that the hill rumbles with disdain for the filling of roles. The circles tighten and the land beneath the land screams out its desires. It is so that they are fated to arrive, once more, at the place of doors.

## 48. Kali and Child lying under a tree.

"It's a strange thing to be rotting under a tree, waiting for a new narrator to continue our story."

Kali acts as a broken toy at times; the child knows this. She is a makeshift thing, clockwork in need of winding.

"Indeed, but rotting is our nature, after all. I wonder if John will realize this before more of us die?"

"He will see, eventually. All shadows eventually give way to light."

"You speak wisely, Kali. Now, let us get back to being dead. All this talk is making me feel enlivened."

"Yes, now back to the land of the dead. Let us rot under our beautiful tree."

## 49. Shade.

They walk, hand in hand, to the outskirts of the town. They walk to a place that only John has seen, the site of recent tragedy.

It is a place of emptiness.

It is a place bereft of motion.

It is a place where the promises of a new growth are the faintest embers under a weight of ash.

Maggie is enrapt in John's telling of the months that have past. She is enamored again in the scent of her old lover. The sky is thrown with waves of violet, as the lovers once again claim rights to themselves.

He lets her lead, knowing the way will be true. John is convinced of Maggie's renewed claim into his world, and she of his to hers.

They are again bound, and now by name.

They are again the Lovers. A tarot deck painted into the ephemeral concept of life.

In the woods, Kali waits, fading slightly in the gathering dark.

Maggie gestures to what appears to her an unkempt Victorian in a patch of brown grass, set off from the road.

"John, that house over there. It reminds me of your office."

"Ah, yes, similar indeed. I had assumed you'd find it. That is our destination."

She taps his arm lightly, “Oh? Is that a satellite location? You guys franchising out?”

“I suppose it is a satellite locality. But, alas, there is no franchise… yet. If you will take upon you the honorific of manager, you will be its caretaker. Care to try it on?”

“Of course. Honestly, I'm relieved. With your birds and dogs, and moving trees, I was expecting something more uncomfortable.”

“Good. I was unsure. It's an odd request… I suppose.”

“You've dragged me across town with tales of sentient trees and shadows which intend to kill me. I think a leisurely visit to an old house isn't too much to ask at this point.”

They walk across the yellowed lawn.

John shivers looking at the poorly filled holes, thinking of fresh graves where trees once took root. He sees Maggie staring at them as well, as if by a nascent mimicry she feels, with him, the anguish of the fallen.

The whimsy of the day has dropped, and she holds his hand tighter as they pass the rounded graves. They approach the hallway of doors, and he looks to her for guidance. The shattered windowsill pays silent testimony to his last visit.

“Which door is it?”

“Well, that's for you to decide. I think that's why we're here.”

“Well, if I were the entrance to this place I'd be the door over there, the one with the red handle.”

“Let's see,” he smiles to himself as the door opens without protest.

She has chosen well.

The house welcomes her as owner.

The house blesses John's return with the orange glow of renewed faith.

She leads him inside, studying the layout.

The couch bristles and she turns to it, recognizing it from the other office.

She sees the peeling paint, the lithographs on the walls from years forgotten. The floors are strewn with newspaper and the flotsam and jetsam of ages gone by. She looks in silence, and John follows.

He feels her radiate. He feels her welcoming grace.

This place, so newly broken, is completed again with her entry.

Across the town and under the hill, an incensed scream is echoing towards the void. The denizens of the other place will rail against the completed circles of the peripheral.

"I love it."

"I hoped that you would say that. This place is joyous with your arrival."

"So, what do we do now?"

"Well, I believe that you simply live here. Be a caretaker of an abandoned point in the map of the periphery. I do not think there's much more to it than that. Simply exist until I finish with my work. Then, I suppose we'll know enough to introduce you to the other sight."

"So, I'm to wait here while you go off to that place on the hill? That seems a little bit pointless doesn't it? What part do I play in all this?"

He realizes that the awareness of the periphery, the joy and the horrors, the crawling sense of fate, is enough to keep him moving… but what of her? He realizes that he must consult Kali and the child, read through the remaining manuscripts of the generation now completely gone. He must know what Maggie's role will be.

“I don't know, to be honest,” he says, taking her hand in his, “but I will find out. Wait here for a bit and I will go back to the woods. Avoid doors save for the one we entered. Make no new doors until you have the powers to do such. Laugh and bring joy back to this dusty shell. Live as you would anywhere else, and you will be fine.”

# 50. The Sun, *ex post facto.*

In the past, when dreams were still at a premium and the wails of strife had yet been brought forth through the actions of John the Elder, a man named John and a man named Hephaestus sat in comfortable chairs, spinning yarns about the years to come.

In the chair, on the left, sat a thin and attractive man, with leg crossed over the other, a cigar burning in the dish to his right. Also to his right, existed another man, slightly stockier and just as tall. In the air before his face was an exhalation of purple smoke.

"Hephaestus my boy, I believe we will start that location you spoke of. Why not take our battle to the hills themselves? We shall blaze a trail of righteousness through the woods and upon the highest peak. We will open a place of wonders. Of sights and perceptions so deviously tiny that the shivering masses of the other side will nary brave enter."

"John, my dearest and eldest friend, you speak as prophecy, a blessing indeed in these lovely days! What shall we call this wonderland upon the hill?"

John, grinned mischievously, "Well, it would be the JBW Estates, Corp. of course!"

"Ha-ha! Very well done, indeed. John Bradley Weishaupt, you shall be upon the hill in both *nominus* and practice. Well done, indeed!"

"Thank you my eldest friend, Hephaestus, first of his generation. Tell me, when do you suppose we move to the place on the hill? Tell me, when do you suppose we move to the other side once more? When do we take back what was ours?"

"John, my dearest, I believe we will take the hill as soon as we can draft the proper paper work. We shall march upon that den of previous villainy and false prophets and plant new seedlings as soon as we feel comfortable. I shall call upon Dura and Gideon, the lovers in the South, for help."

"Prudent, but unnecessary. Between the two of us, the vibrations of our sight will clear that place within moments. But if you should like them to come along, the more, the merrier! Now, on to the greater point. The other place. How long till we join with them again?"

"John, I believe we will have long lives upon this plane. We will have healthy trees and nightly dancing. I believe that we will be called into that place as the last two of our generation. As Gideon the elder and Kali of the shared visions were the last of theirs, handing me the mantle of manager of this place upon their fertilizing of The Tree."

"Hephaestus, my boy, that is forever from now. Let us take back the other side before we join it permanently. Let us look upon the rift that our predecessors tore and heal it with the gentle caresses of our awareness."

"John, let us first take the hill. Then, and only when we are comfortable with the expansion, shall we consider melding the two worlds. We need more bodies, more energy awareness, for the sacrament to take place. Let us hire new people to spread my gospel. I shall write more books and call upon more names. Let us meld this world enough to allow for the acceptance of the other. Let us give new names to these ancient woods."

John sat, passively annoyed, his cigar left burning in the ashtray. He leaned over towards Hephaestus and placed his hand upon his.

"Hephaestus, you are far too short-sighted. We are the bringers of the new peace. We are the managers for a new world.

Yes. We shall take my hill. Then, we shall find new names. We will find even more places to make our own. But I will have that world, Hephaestus. We shall form this reality to suit our perceptions. We shall heal them, and make them know the truth, if there can be truth."

"You are too impatient, I should say. You know as well as I what the one who once held my name did. You know the weight of that rift and of the broken worlds sits upon my shoulders, *in nominus*. We cannot force this issue. We shall spread the word. We shall bring in new blood. But we will wait till the proper time. There is no need to rush ourselves into further mistakes. Let the birds have it till it is time for both of us to move on, no sooner."

John grimaced at the utterance of the birds. He shot a look at his manager and friend, and with a forced calmness stood up.

"Hephaestus, we take the hill tomorrow. I shall become its master. Then, I will bridge the worlds. There are no more words for now. I shall see you soon."

"I hope upon hope that you reconsider. Good evening my eldest friend."

## 51. The Chariot.

In the office, in the woods, John paces nervously. In his room, in the office, in the woods, he thinks of Maggie surrounded by doors, and of Kali with her animal prowling. He sees the changes in the two of them since Maggie's arrival. The child in the yard is now the child upstairs. He ignores The Tree, now brown with rot. John knows something must be done. John knows he must take back the hill and somehow stop the Elder. He paces until the child enters.

"John the Younger, Keeper of the hill and manager in name, I have a request of you."

"Anything you'd like."

"I believe that in order to survive the trial on the hill you must first walk where your predecessor walked before you. The work will be better if you enter the periphery in body as well as sight. You must cross where it is not safe to cross."

"Enter the periphery? So far as I've understood, it is parallel with this place. How do we enter someplace we're already in? I thought we lived in the periphery, but it took training and effort to see it."

"That is exactly truth, John the Younger. Yet it is also completely false. The world as it was is this one, though slipped to the side, hidden. We of the sight can look and see the shadow shapes of that place that was. We of the sight can render an effect upon it, if we so choose. But we are not there in body, fully. Think of it as a mirror. Our reflection is on the mirror, in the mirror: but we are not the mirror. We cast a reflection and change the view, but we are not there. The periphery is the land on which the reflection lays, not the thing from which it is cast."

"So, we are in the other place, but only as a trick of vision. We are both there and here, but more here than... this is difficult."

"It is not. Your predecessor saw it and walked it. I will take you there and you will understand. If you are him, and him you, we will be safe. You see, John the Elder was one of the few who could walk, unimpeded, in the old place. He could take things there and bring them back again. So, we will walk in those lands as he once did, and see what can still be seen. We will visit the once and forever land under and upon the hill and talk to the man who holds his name for too long. We will demand an audience and an explanation. We will seek counsel with the allies of the other place if they still draw breath. John the Younger, today we will walk where our ancestors fell. Today we enter the periphery."

He looks upon the aged child in trust and amazement. John has come to realize that the periphery is much more than a subtle amusement, a parlor trick or idle philosophy. He knows that where he walks, he enacts upon that place something permanent; and that where he has gone is but a sliver of what is available. He thinks of the faces in the whiskey, of the angels and the dead in his dreams. He knows that to follow the child into the other place could be his end. But, he now knows that to not follow would be death. He has accepted his role in this trans-dimensional play, and is resolute to finish it well.

"I would love to walk with you in the lands of our ancestors. How do we proceed?"

"I knew you would come. I have provisions packed and have informed the esteemed Kali of our departure. She wishes you kindnesses and love on your journey and regrets her absence on the day of your transposition into the other. But she is losing what was her basic nature in order to take on the major aspects of the coming other. She is afraid to see you till completion. Follow me."

"She's what?"

"I will explain when the time is right. For now, let us walk into the woods. The path will be where you last left it, when you were not you and the Trees were yet joyous."

They exit the office through the back door, a traditional affair free from the complex traps and ornamentation often found there . The child exits first, then John. Walking upon the yard they see it is dying. The Tree sad and drooping, a moan in the air, the sway of limbs in mournful breezes.

"It's rotting."

"Indeed. They drink from bad springs and draw dark air. The loss of Dura and Gideon has set into motion the end of this iteration. The things under the hill are pressing to burn this place soon."

"It's sick. I can feel them writhing."

"Indeed. Let us set to moving. The path is ahead and it is long. Let us take the time needed and no more. The Trees will stand for a while yet. We will walk to ensure the hill will be taken and the Trees spread to new grounds. Follow."

The path through the woods runs from directly behind the once powerful tree, a line of jagged rocks and red soil cutting into the depths of the forest. The child walks and John follows. John recognizes this place. He looks to his feet moving and sees a part of the past he does not experience directly. He walks in the steps of his previous self, and each step brings him closer to where he, as the Elder, went wrong.

The woods are quiet, except for the susurration of the trees and the gravel crunch of footfalls. Nearly hypnotized by the rhythmic steps and lulling breeze, they walk the path as if it were the existent world compressed to a point, and extended, on the ground, in a forest, moving further and farther into the darkness ahead.

The sky rolls forward as in stop motion. The breezes move with speeds unbecoming of their impact. They, the two seers, slide through the woods as if forgetting gravity and the subtler laws of motion and entropy. They fall into a sleep walk as the sounds of crunching footfalls interact with the swaying trees. The screech of a swooping bird reverberates through the woods, waking them from their dream. Shaking their heads clear of the hypnagogia they had wandered in for the past hours, days, weeks, moments, they stop to look.

The trees are now a scraggly tangle of brush and ash. The sky is yellow and stained, the sun red and sputtering. The child turns and whispers,

“We are here.”

John feels this place within him, a nervous recognition of whatever may have came before.

He feels the loss of this place, forcing his reactions down as he pushes forward.

He knows this is the true home, even as perverted and wrong as it sits now.

He recognizes the pure land of who came before.

The forest hates itself for what it has become.

The twisted visions from the other side cannot do justice to the loss and hate of the place.

The men of knowing hate themselves for leaving the forest.

The shadows of the periphery drink heavily from the guilt and discomfort a generation gone to soil have wrought.

The sky, rent in two, is a billowing ribbon of black in the sepia pollution.

The ruins of a once perfect place litter the ground, broken marble going to dust.

They walk on the crunching matter of generations gone to

ruin, the ribbon of black, writhing snake-like, the ground reflecting the rift in darkened grasses and rusted remnants.

The man and the boy who would be man walk on the land of the living past, the echo of what should have been, if not for the failed will of the previous.

"I know this place. This was home."

"You see correctly. This is the physical aspect of the corruption of the once pure land. Our assumption proves true; you can walk here without insult. The forest finds you as welcome as you seem to find it. Look behind you. You will see the fractured land from which we came."

Behind him John sees a dried-out forest, burnt, dying, cold. Above the dead forest the shape of a house manifests, translucent and vague. It is the office, though intangible… more so an implied state than a physical one. As they approach, the house gains the aspect of this place; as they approach the office shifts perspective with each step.

He sees the animal nature of the Trees, the glowing aspects of looking into the periphery. It is angelic and ephemeral, solid yet unreal.

It is the point of bisection between the world as known and the world as perceived. The office sits as matrix between perceptions. Its existence is reliant on the distracted eyes of the rational world, and the raw perception of the seers of the periphery, as well as the abstractions within it.

In the window moves the shape of Kali, be-winged and hideous. She is leather and filth, a decaying mass of reptile and human. Standing with her is a half-dead child, a face of rot, a body decomposing.

He sees the house as a writhing organic entity, bent in mimicry of a structure now so far away.

The water closet of the rational world is a pond in this place.

The pond is a house of animals only seen through the corners and the indistinct places between awareness and sleep.

The Tree fights against its chains.

The reptile bleeds in the places of its holding.

Where exists in the other place an entrance, a slide, a set of stairs, there sits sculpture left in disrepair; there sits painting half covered, and of course, the all pervasive ruins from the time before. The ruins are strewn like leaves, like placeholders of a civilization once alive, once vibrant, now left to disrepair.

From the corner of this ramshackle reflection, a half-shadow strides forth, a shimmering mirage walking in both life and death, in memory and creation.

It is moving, yet somehow inanimate; it is, or was, the aspect once introduced as Hephaestus James Bonobus, the lost father in John's fantasy. John and the child stand, stunned, ashamed of the work that has passed since his departure. He approaches.

"Welcome, my children. I am glad for your company, especially in such an esteemed state as you occupy. The living of your place rarely tread upon these tired grounds. Before we begin, you should know that I have forgiven you both. John and The Child. John knows not what he does in that semi-light place. Child, your work has failed, and I forgive you for it. This was a trying time, and mistakes are to be expected. Please, walk well in this place of neither possibility."

The Child is the first to speak, "I had feared you would be here. Always the worker, never the Saint. Hello, my oldest friend."

They try to embrace and the thing that was Hephaestus passes through The Child.

"Oh, I had forgotten that little problem. I am sorry Child, but the world does not work as it once did."

"Hello, Sir. You were missed. Thank you for your

forgiveness."

"John the Younger! You seem stronger now than when I left. Blessings be unto you both. Now, let me get to speaking, for the time of our reunion is nearly at an end. John, and Keeper, I grant you permission to take back the Elder. Your words will be your first onslaught. When they fail, and they will, take him to The Tree; return him home. I have grown tired and reminiscent in the long days since my departure. Any company would be welcome. Go find the small ones, they will lead you to the creatures of the upper order who will grant you passage. I must return now, for the business of miming your world is calling. Be well my friends, I shall return to you when the opportunity for more work presents itself."

And with that, he shimmers and fades back into the ephemeral office. He returns to the maybe-state of possibility that sits on the spinning edge of theory and philosophy.

## 52. Uttering the world into existence.

In front of a nearly invisible structure, The Child and John stand.

The sketch-like house sits in conflict with reason. Its lines and contours are moving, swaying in the nonsense physics of a world gone to madness.

"John the Younger, what you see now is the world you knew, as seen through the suppositional filter that is the periphery," The Child stands, looking into the eyes of John, both pupil and master. "This is a universe free from the fetters of time and identity. We just spoke to the origin point of whom we knew, in that place, as Hephaestus James Bonobus. We are in a place that sits very close to a true state… or as close as can be approached to a state nearing truth. From a specific angle, the house is the manifestation of what goes on inside. This is the map of a territory long since past. This place is the manifestation of what has taken root. This place is the echo of the fall waiting to be silenced. We, John the Younger, are the makers of that silence. If the work is good and the vision pure, we all shall return, and this place will blossom with the joys known before."

"And where are the things which breach through to the place from where we came? Where are the murderous shadows and the small things that feed the Trees? This place seems as dead to them as it became to our kind."

"A fine question… one for which I have no answer. They do exist here, but their numbers remain relatively low for the destruction wrought. Hephaestus had a theory that in order for this place and the other to coexist, there must be a balance struck. Our ancestors took root too quickly and took too much. They made the choices that lead us to this horrific point. He believed that when enough of us enter this place they will be forced back into theirs; an equilibrium will be created. Peace will occur, and the ruins will rise up as they were… the sky will be sutured… the Trees will happily recreate themselves, and their smaller ones will again exist in numbers."

"Where do we begin?"

"We find the offspring of the ones who remain here from before. The Elder John came back with stories of the elder ones still living in the small spaces left behind. We will set out to find them, to ask them their advice. I believe we follow the rift. The rift will show us the way."

"Indeed."

## 53. The other way too.

"Hello? Child in the yard? John? Girl with the dress? Anyone home?"

Maggie has been led to the office by notions unknown.

Sitting in the drawing room in the place of doors, she came to realize that she must visit the office in the woods. Maggie has been moving at the end of her strings, down the familiar roads into the woods. She must speak to someone about her duties, her watch. She feels the pang of responsibility as she walks from the place of doors to the office in the woods.

And so Maggie stands in the doorway of an office, waiting for another set to be built, another room in the growing playhouse of the periphery.

Kali appears in the doorway, back-lit by that familiar sepia light. The scene begins. The strings of the marionettes are tightly wound upon expert fingers.

"Maggie of the place of doors, welcome. I am Kali of the desk, watcher of this place until such time that one or the other returns to his position. Please be welcome in this place. Know that it, and myself, welcome you as both sister and coworker, a sacred position."

"Thank you, Kali of the desk. I am glad to finally make your acquaintance."

They sit on opposing couches, between them a table of ancient stained wood holds a tray of tea and small cookies. Kali had been expecting this.

"Please, drink from our tea, eat from our plate. It is the way of treating guests preferred by the followers of The Tree."

"Oh, thank you."

Maggie lifts her cup, as does Kali.

Kali stares over the lip of her cup forcing an intense eye contact.

They place their cups down in silent unison.

They, in perfect sync, pick up a cookie, lifting them as if connected by unseen wires.

Kali maintains her contact and Maggie's discomfort turns into acceptance, as if they had been in that same room forever.

Maggie feels Kali within her, as if they had sat together since time began.

They eat in synchronized bites and smile in fleeting moments.

So they sit, locked within themselves until the tea grows cold, and the day slips into night. Maggie's awareness is transiting from that deep spin of confusion into the steadied calm of acceptance, of knowledge. Kali, smirking in accomplishment of something so long in the planning, breaks the spell by the clinking of porcelain on porcelain.

"Thank you for joining me. What brings you to us this day, Maggie of the doors?"

"I don't know, to be honest. It simply popped into my head that I needed to be here. It occurred to me that I need an explanation as to what I'm supposed to do at that place. This seemed the only option for answers."

"Well, dearest one, you are to replace Gideon. He fell from our story some years past, and has recently reentered the cycle.

You are to be the one in the place of doors, as I will replace Dura. We are to be wed, in a sense. You will take, for the briefest moment, the mantle of Maggie of the Pairing."

"Wed?"

"Yes. But not in that way. You see… it is done already. We have performed the ceremony of tea and sacred bread. The Tree is now within you; as I am within the tree; as we all are bound to the service of this place. I am sorry for not explaining beforehand, but it does not work in that way. We are entwined now, like molecules, like lovers in tangled sheets, or strong breezes, the zephyrs of spring."

"I do feel a great fondness for you, Kali. I feel like we've known each other for years."

"Well stated Maggie. We have known each other for as long as the soil has had the nutrients to sustain our kind. We have known each other for as long as the locus of the sacred fruit stretches back and ahead through this place. Please, try to remember yesterday."

"We were in… oh… it's… it's like stereo."

"Yes. And so it is that you pass from that other place of routine, from the strangle hold of linear progress, to this one of the unplanned, of the quantum. Welcome to the company and to our newly shared past. We are now bound. You in the place of doors, and me in the auspice of John the Younger. You were brought to us through him for this purpose. Welcome, my love."

"I am not me. But I am not you. I remember with glimpses of both. I am a seer of the other place yet it is clouded, dream-like. I know the feeling of blood rushing from that other place, into this one. I sense the pulsing veins leading into the Tress, and the rot growing upon them. Kali, I can feel my home calling to me, the doors are crying out. I can see his mistake. Gideon did not understand. Gideon did not see properly."

## 54. Where once stood Gideon and Dura, The Lovers in sepia.

Back in time, before relativity, before any of this was invented, Dura and Gideon lived in a wondrous place of infinite doors. They often took communion with The Tree and tasted its flesh. They luxuriated in all the comforts of the followers of the periphery.

Back in time, a man lived in a fantastic castle upon a hill, or so he saw it. Another man lived in a shining house in a fantastic wood. They often met over tea, and the still ubiquitous fruit.

Back in time, a man in a high castle broke certain vows and hoarded certain objects.

A man in the woods chastised and spoke at length his philosophies.

A couple in a place of doors and vortices amused themselves away from the conflict. They began to leave more and more doors open. The couple in the place of doors forgot that their creations ever existed.

The man sat blissful in his place of doors. The woman watched passively as the place turned from destination to journey, from position to superposition.

Until one day that the man in the woods called upon his friends at the place of doors to help him with a problem upon the hill. Dura came running, knowing that the evil growing upon the hill must be stopped. Gideon sat in idle amusement, placid in his place of doors.

It was then that Hephaestus James Bonobus and Dura, once of the place of doors, walked into the place upon the hill. It was then that they declared their friend a traitor. It was then that they proclaimed his work as poorly done… as evil.

It was then, that a man declared himself as Elder until the end of days.

After the glow of once upon a time had dissipated, Dura left the hill, spiraling down into the woods. Upon her landing, she took up the top floor of an oddly proportioned house in a swath of woods, forswearing the doors of her youth until he called upon her once again.

Gideon forgot his dear Dura and grew older and older; allowing himself to become enamored by increasing novelty; letting his trees grow sick, eventually uprooted by storm.

John forgot Hephaestus and grew greedier, lusting after a longer life and the dominion over the seers of the sight.

Hephaestus was heart sick, broken, a giant in wait for someone or something to release him from the coils binding him to the linear earth.

# 55. In this style, 10/6.

"Kali, my lover and dearest friend, thank you for this gift."

Kali and Maggie stare with empty eyes into one another.

"I will lock the unnatural ones and create the supports for what is to come: The new paths of the new generation. Let us burn the memories of those who failed before and cast them asunder. Thank you for your gift Kali, my dearest."

"And I thank you for mine. The dialog is complete. You are now part of here and there, the same as I. We speak with the voice of the periphery, and the sights as yet unknown. When their campaign ends and the Elder is gone, we shall sing with joyous songs of pairing. We shall dance with abandon under trees, verdant and sated. I thank you again Maggie of the Doors, Maggie of the shared past."

"And I thank you Kali of the desk, Kali of shared hearts. Treat him well, and make him understand that it is not I who has left, but that I have undergone this thing which was destined since before the sky was split. Thank you, my dearest. We shall celebrate soon."

So it is that the new generation pairs.

The childhood rags of the earthly realm are cast aside.

The place of doors glows with the powers of the woods.

The earth will soon take seed… or become fallow.

Maggie of the place of doors will stand strong against the one whose greed took him underground and away from the cycle of pairing and rebirth.

And so it is that the staff strengthens.

And so it is that they who venture forth find the path to something long since left behind.

## 56. The void.

It is in the woods, in the periphery, that the child and man walk. They follow a broken sky into broken trees.

They walk with an expectation of something dark hanging over them.

The children of ancient trees run through the small paths between bushes.

They skip in wooden motions, echoing the movements of what came before.

They are but automatons performing the motions of the days of blood and life.

They are marionettes on the strings of history, robotic movements in the darkness of the past.

They skip past a startled John and a relieved child. The child thanks the higher thoughts that the children still exist, still play the roles of the previous ones. They are the hope of the new plantings, the fading souls in the minimal movements of an uncaring and increasingly entropic universe. They recognize the pair in the woods as part of the cycle to which they are bound, and so ignore their trespasses into the territory of the lesser and greater. They smile internally and hope, in ritual, that they will be freed and allowed into the land of the growing, the hidden spaces at the edges of themselves that demarcate the world as perceived by us. They run with rusted motion through the branches and under the maze of tangled grass, disappearing into the mounds of ceramic and mud, which dot the landscape.

"What are those things?"

"They are the abandoned children. They are the woods left to rot. They are what we follow to find our friends; whom, thanks to our departed Hephaestus, are known to still exist as far as existence can be judged by our broken eyes. They are the Seedlings of the lesser trees, gone these long years."

The child glows radiant with newfound hope of a better tomorrow. He has not seen the seedlings for too long. His warmth of gratitude draws them back, like open fires on cold nights.

"Look, they are coming. They're, like…" John grasps at the right words to describe the creatures. "…like, little tree… people. Kali would love this."

The seeds point their wooden eyes at John and with vegetable utterance sing greetings.

John is shocked at the hideousness of their voice, if it could be called a voice. They speak like the noise of machines seizing, lubricated with sap and rust.

Their utterances stab into John in lightning flashes into his chest. In his recoil, his immediate revulsion, a note of intrigue is sprung. He has dreamt of that sound before. He has heard it in the wails of the balloons entering the ravenous Tree.

"They sing you their greetings. You should greet them back."

"How do I greet them?"

"Just as you would The Tree in the yard or the form that was He."

John approaches with as much caution politeness allows.

The tiny wooden things stand, their faces set as sculpture.

"Hello, my new friends in this ancient place. I am called John the Younger. I bring you greeting from myself, and from myself as the head of the HJ Bonobus Corporation. We are at your service."

With their unison voice they sing like screeching anarchy. "Thank you John the Younger. We, the seedling, are at yours. May we speak with minds? This method proves ill-met."

"Of course."

He turns to the child, and in a whisper, asks what is meant by speaking with minds. In his head he hears a heavenly choir.

"We have little use for the articulations of man in these long days since we rose from root. We sing better to the base of your system, not the *vox*. What brings such illustrious guests to this place? It has been long since one such as yourself walked with the radiance of friendship into this place."

The Child steps forward, moving with his eerie, preternatural grace, "We seek the remaining friends of the old ways. We must find the one who keeps my name too long. We must plead with him to stop his ways and return to the cycle with which we all must return."

"You will fail in your pleadings. But we believe your work is good, and will show you the way to the remains of what came before. Only a few of the parents remain in a state that would prove useful to you. Be aware that they have no love for your worlds since the one who bears your sigil used this place for sport and greed. Please, follow us into the smaller places. We will accommodate your stature as we go. They await your arrival with bated breath and sharpened knives. Speak with truth and ignore the trifling novelties which have thus far proved the undoing of the endeavor that is the human place."

So they follow, child and man, running swiftly behind wooden dolls in sequence. Small gaps in the underlying brush open wide as they approach. The twisted bramble unties into doorways, into darker places hiding in the desiccated trees.

They follow for what appears to them as hours, what to the other place are days.

The sun moving like a stop motion film, stifled rhythmically as it passes through the rift.

They run with legs and lungs replenished from the waves of geometric energies that are flowing up from the undulating earth.

John and child move as speed; they move as motion. They travel as if by description of movement rather than by the physical actions being performed.

The motions of the plants, the undulations of the land, the rhythm of the sky all sing in concert with the beating of John's heart.

The seedlings, untiring, move swiftly with a magnetic grace and unfaltering confidence.

They move as the sun arcs across the sky, behind the rift, and again, a daily eclipse of gray. The Trees thin. The paths grow to suit the human sized travelers, now moving as machines.

They stop.

John, towering above the children, both of flesh and of wood, takes deep breathes of the cold, clean, air. In a clearing from the bramble, the small marionettes look to John with their obsidian eyes, signaling arrival.

The angelic noise of their communication breaks the silence.

"This is where we part ways, John the Younger and young master Keeper."

"Thank you for your guidance and company," The Child speaks in the salesman tones of the late Hephaestus. "This would have proved impossible without your help."

"Indeed, The Child speaks truth. I thank you as well," John falls into cadence with The Child. "If I may ask just one more thing, what are we supposed to do now?"

"You wait; they arrive. The air speaks of the coming of something ancient. Be well, we shall be there to cultivate when this ends. Watch for us when the Elder falls, and your vision is mended."

The Child, the Younger, and the wooden ones stand in a crude circle, quiet in farewell. The humans nod and the seedlings bow awkwardly, and so slip back into the woods of the other place, tiny vegetable martyrs of the periphery.

"So we wait?"

"Indeed. We wait."

# 57. So it goes.

In the place of doors, Maggie holds an imaginary string, and with a sigh, releases. She watches the windows sit patiently, crying to herself.

The windows are dusty and without light. She turns from them and, red eyed, she walks into the sitting room, waiting for tea that will never come.

Kali takes up a balloon, one of the remaining few in the months since the child and John had disappeared, and lets it be fed to The Tree. The Tree's movements are slow and the balloon is taken into the boughs, a flow of red and black washes down its trunk; it cries silently in pain.

Kali's tears stream down as she returns to the house, knowing there is nothing that can be done.

The office is quiet, and Kali walks the grounds. The place of doors is quiet and Maggie walks the grounds.

The nights now constantly disrupted by the Elder's calling. Their nights disrupted by the perversions of the hill.

From the hill there is a constant clamor, metal crashing and the primal screams of what lives below. The remaining trees cower in fear of the coming death, their rot visible, their end eminent.

In the office, Kali stares at her screen and mimes typing, as Maggie taps out a short letter to the parents she left behind.

The Tree in the yard is forever emanating discomfort.

The walls of the office are forever taking that spoiled energy, forcing it throughout its reaches. The place is black with the losses of the past.

The woods turn to the color of rust.

The remnants of the previous iterations are less visible than the year previous. Certain doors fall out of favor and existence.

The thing under the hill laughs as his seat grows more permanent.

# 58. Drawing symbols in the dirt.

In a world formed by the machinations of minds long since passed, a man and a child exist in a muted grace. In a world created by the pressure waves of probability vibrating forth from the minds of broken men, a child and a man wait in a circle barren of trees. They wait, surrounded by the ever-present chunks of marble, remnants of the ancient statuary formed in the imaginations of creators yet to be invented. In a world darkened by a black rift in the ever shifting sky, the probability wave of existence is about to collapse under observation of something impossible.

In the dirt, the child traces glyphs of calling, protection, and harmony.

The man taps his foot and exhales.

The air vibrates, and the lull is ceased.

The runes of the child glow like fading fire, as John becomes aware again.

"What are those?" he asks pointing to the scrawls in forest floor.

"These are part of our history. They are part of your history. They are a means of gaining awareness of your inner workings. They were handed down as the walls began to fall to ruin. These were formed in the time of the first upheaval of the woods… the burning. I draw the figure to protect us; I draw the circle to declare peace between our perceptions; I draw the bird to tell them that we come with the friendship of the old ways."

"Who is it that we are waiting for?"

"The birds," The Child motions to his crude scribbles. "We await the birds."

## 59. Yet another, and equally valid, way to view this whole thing.

In the woods, a man eats from sealed-packets and wanders soundlessly, watching over a child, as perceived, at his side. He sees the woods as ancient and full of ruins from a fictional place, fallen in a bygone epoch.

In this state, he has walked in elaborate circles.

In this state, he has fed from the woods and the waning provisions of home.

In the woods, a man wanders with glazed over eyes and frothing mouth, speaking to birds and drawing in the sand.

In the woods, a play is acted, and acted again.

In the woods, the words are spoken, and spoken again as they were spoken in that other place.

He sees the other place, and walks, miming curiously the motions of the internal.

The sees that other place, and gesticulates to the boughs and to the sky.

He sees that other place, as time passes in the motions of shadows moving across the pine needle floor.

## 60. Super Ego.

The child and the man sit, back to back, in the center of crudely drawn circle. The ruins of what came before are strewn across their respective fields of vision.

They look to the marred sky and fall into the shadowy recesses.

They sing songs to each other full of words with no meaning, carrying no significance.

The glyphs sinking deeper into the earth under the broken sky as they look to the rift and see it move, shifting like oil in waves.

And from the great fissure is issued a wave of sketches, outlines, shadows, placeholders in motion. They coalesce in thronging motions, spin and swoop across the stained sky. They, looking like a charcoal rubbing on trace paper, somehow move in three dimensions. The swell of blackness brings itself into the circle in which the humans stand, and from this mass three shapes disseminate. Three nearly-human forms take shape.

"The Oriphiel. A race of ascended masters far older than our kind. They are akin to the early animal god worshiped in years long past. We call them the birds. They come from a place far outside our ken. Though we have traveled together for what seems to us a great distance, they only have to shift slightly to reach this place."

The Birds speak in symphony, they speak like throat singing and the subtle strings behind great movements.

"We are well met, our friends from below. We speak to you as before, and hope this method still suits you."

John stands back, breaking from his focus. Shaking his head clear, he cries out to no one:

"Birds, human birds? No! I just ran after tree children to meet Bird Gods? This is not… no. Gods in the form of birds… in the form of humans? Half visible dogs and strange balloons…. I can take those. Those are metaphor, visual aids in a search. But, this, this is… this is madness. I've gone mad… again. Too much, this is too much."

He looks to his side to find The Child is missing.

He looks forward to find no angels, no birds, no devils in the trees.

He stands, alone, cold, in a valley of newer growth, "The Burned-Over District."

He looks again to the void at his side, a sheen of normalcy and common sight sit in muted testimony to a Buddha-like child's existence.

The subtle movements of branches are from the wind.

The ground is firm in new frost.

He speaks to no one:

"All I wanted was a job. A simple job… a desk, some lights, a boss with annoying quirks and maybe a coffee mug. What now? I'm a fucking lunatic lost in the woods. Lost. Where the hell is the kid?"

As if answering him, a faint voice echoes wordlessly from the trees.

"Wonderful. It was fun. A great fat guy with a weird philosophy. It made sense. It's like East Coast Zen; just look out the sides of your eyes and see the universe for the fraud that it is!

Fun times, cute girls in nice dresses! Now Maggie is wrapped up in this nonsense… I think. Is she? How the hell can Maggie be at a place full of doors? Did she even agree to go? Why did I leave her in the first place? It's just a long foggy hall for the past months. What the hell have I become?"

He paces the pine needles. He slaps bark in unison with his points.

"Cassiel is gone, missing. The fat man is dead. The old people are dead. I'm in the fucking woods, all alone, talking to fucking trees!" he screams, "TREES!"

He is walking towards the child's meek beckoning.

"Now what? I find my metaphorical father and kill him to prevent something I don't even understand the half of? Listen. This is wisdom. What is wisdom? What the hell were those things? What am I listening to? Have I finally gone over the edge? But Hephaestus was real; Hephaestus understood. He understood and I bathed in his blood. That forgiveness from him cannot have come from me. This must have a basis in reality."

Kicking at dirt, he moves through the coniferous and oak. He walks and spits, screaming at times.

"This must be a kind of walking meditation. It's the only explanation. The child is obviously some kind of savant Buddhist, who has, over time, taught me this periphery thing. There is no evil, no dogs in the shadows, no demons in the trees. There must not be. It's a metaphor, has to be. There were no doppelgangers and demigods. There must not have been a shadow of an older me preying on the office. The Child, he's only a kid; The Tree, the tree is just a… Oh god The Tree. He rained. It rained him. I need to go home; I have no home… I live in an office. How the hell did I end up living in an office? A few months ago I was a regular guy… shitty apartment, no job, great girlfriend. What the hell happened? Was she right about Hephaestus? Am I in a cult? He can't be evil. He is too happy in his little sins to be actually evil. Oh god Maggie. Does she even know what we've seen here? HE RAINED

DOWN ON US! Oh Christ I'm going to be sick."

He walks, head down. He is walking towards the office, towards the voice of The Child. Sirens float in the air echoing from the distant town, traveling in the scent of unseen smoke.

He sees the small thing sitting Buddha on the ground, drawing circles in the dirt.

"Hello John. Finished with your tantrum I see?”

"Hello Child. I needed a moment to think. Are you okay?"

"John, you have broken the covenant. We must return and beg their forgiveness. This insult would have proven deadly in the ancient days. But in those long years since last we lived together with the beings of the other side, the laws have slackened, the judgments more lax. We must go back and beg forgiveness. We must ask them for permission to end this thing permanently. This error must be righted, and soon."

"Child. I need to sleep in a bed right now. I need food. I don't know what's going on right now, but I can tell you it will not be going on in these woods. Let us set our feet to moving."

"But John the Younger, bringer of…"

"Enough. Listen to me kid, I'm the adult here. You and I both are going back to that office and I'm going to figure out what exactly is going on. Then, and only then, will I entertain another idea for a field trip. Understood?"

"You don't sound like yourself, John the Younger. I must talk to The Tree about this."

"Good. I'm going to take a shower and sleep, for once, without ghosts.”

They turn towards the office, walking in a lifeless arbor.

## 61. Gnosis(A Greek chorus).

In a sea of black, motions ripple in the shape of men. In a dark space, faceless masses sway back and forth, fall and reform like waves in oil.

**Hephaestus James Bonobus**: In the woods, a man and a child walk. In the woods, our dreams take shape.

**John the Elder**: In the office, another possibility is manifest. In the office, the music is yet plentiful.

**Hephaestus James Bonobus**: In the office, John and Kali dance in loving circles. In the office, John dances alone as the images of Maggie and Kali flash in violent sequence.

**Dura**: In the way of both options, are lingering memories. In the way of both futures, are doubts from the past.

**Hephaestus James Bonobus**: In the periphery, all things are done at varying paces. In the periphery, all things are moving from finish to start, and back again.

**John the Elder**: In the woods, they move from finish to start. In the woods, they are walking towards a new beginning.

**Dura**: In the woods, a boy and man walk in defiance. In the woods, no one questions the boy.

**Hephaestus James Bonobus**: In the office in the woods, a question will be asked. In the office in the woods, an awareness of generations will form.

**Dura**: In this song, we must give them time and space to act. In this song, we must allow for choice of perception.

**John the Elder**: In the periphery, all things are born of choice. In the periphery, all things are informed by situation.

**Dura**: In the office, he will fall to feverish pieces. In the office, he will become aware.

**John the Elder**: In the way of both, is a ghost of myself. In the way, is a specter of his past.

**Dura**: In that office, the worlds are so near to one another. In that office, the words of the other place are often seen written upon the walls .

**Hephaestus James Bonobus**: Upon the hill, a question was asked. Upon the hill, an answer will be given.

**John the Elder**: On the hill, the other is pacing and planning his movement. On the hill, all things will be done in motion towards the office in the woods.

**Hephaestus James Bonobus**: In the woods, all things will be done, as they have been done. In the woods, all things will be changed in a moment.

**Unison**: In this form, we fall back to the framework of the universe. In this form, we fall.

In a sea of black the waves within the darkness move with entropy. The faceless forms rejoin the oil-black of night. In a sea of dark, all motions cease.

## 62. Cups and Kings, and poorly hidden things.

Upon the doorsteps to the offices of the HJ Bonobus Corp. there's a man dressed in the wardrobe of police. He watches the door swing inward, revealing a woman in a dark dress, looking at him with dead eyes sunken into a porcelain skin.

"Hello ma'am. I'm Detective Wilson. I have a warrant to search the premises. Is John Weishaupt in?"

"No. There is no one by that name here."

"When do you expect him back?"

"As I recently stated, and clearly, there is no one here by that name. Not now, not ever."

The creature once called Kali is furious at the intrusion of this Officer. She is anger unchained, bound with hate for law. She feels her home violated, and this token of order is the offender.

"I know he resides here. I spoke to him a week or so ago. Miss…?"

"I am called Kali of the Desk. Now leave."

"Kali?" His voice is of irritation. He grows tired of these games.

"Yes. Kali is the name I spoke clearly a moment ago. I should think a man of your position would be better trained in the arts of listening. Please, I have much work to do. Please let me be."

"The quicker you tell me where John is today the quicker this will be for both of us. Now, where is John Weishaupt?"

"I have told you already that no one resides here by that name. Your implication that I am lying is something that will not go unpunished." Her teeth are gritted in anger. Her tiny hands are balled into even tinier fists. "Obviously your feet have found purchase in a place unwelcome. Go. Now." Her voice like gravity.

He scans the pages of his notebook furiously in hopes of information which could break this standoff. "John Weishaupt, AKA John the Younger. Does he reside here?"

She turns the switch. "Oh, joyous day! A friend of darling John, please come in and be at peace with this place." Her demeanor moves from violence to exuberance. "You should have told me earlier that you were a friend of John. How silly our little play must seem to those who find joy in such things"

"Oh, thank you, I think. May I enter?"

"Of course. Shed that awful jacket and be at peace. What may I do for you Keeper of the law?"

"As stated, I am looking for John Weishaupt… the Younger. He is needed for questioning in regards to a missing person of his acquaintance. Mr. Cassiel Landry. Now, I have a warrant to search the premises, but it would be much easier and less messy with a nice young lady like you as a guide. Now, do you know his current whereabouts?"

"No. I am afraid he has taken a sabbatical from the HJ Bonobus Corp. The death of our esteemed manager gave him more grief than expected. He is believed to be returning at some point though. I would be glad, and duty bound as secretary, to have him phone you when his arrival is made more physical than this current extemporaneousness. Now. Let's see about your tour."

"Wait, who died?"

"Our manager, Mr. Hephaestus James Bonobus has lost this thread of life."

"I'm sorry to hear that Ma'am. How did it happen?"

"Oh, you know, the passing of ages."

"Ah, yes, of course. Anyway, you have no idea when he will return?"

"Which one?"

"John..." his frustration growing," John the Younger, who else is returning?"

"The child, the one called Hephaestus, The Tree, all of it returns. Please be more specific in your queries."

"Fine. So, John the Younger will be back, and you will have him call this number," He points to the card in his hand.

"How will we know the number when he returns?"

"What?"

"It's on your card. I can't see the point in going to your place of business to look at your card, with no picture I may add, to call you. Seems like a waste of time."

"Stop messing around and take the damn card. This piece of paper allows me full access to this place, but I will not use it for the moment. If I don't hear from Mr. John the Younger in the next few days you best bet that this place will be turned upside down and inside out."

"Oh, that sounds grand. I will wait with bated breath. Good day, constable. I look forward to your next visit. Good day, good days!"

It is then that he finally takes his leave, and she sighs in relief. Hephaestus would be proud, she thinks, as she walks to the basement, returning to the work at hand.

God bless those of the periphery who know how to avoid unwanted looks.

## 63. Bleeding out.

"I am not leaving. I simply need a moment to think. One second I live in poverty, but happily, with a girl to call my own and a rent check due. Next, I'm running after marionettes and listening to houses. I know, I know, Hephaestus did know some things. But he's dead. What the hell? He's dead? I mean, what the hell?"

The Child stands with dead eyes and deaf ears. He looks up at the moving lips of John and waits for the tantrum to end.

"John, the time is nigh. The Elder is heralding in the new age. The things under the hill grow in numbers, the woods are rotting. Now is not the time for a crisis in faith."

"See, this is exactly what I'm talking about! What the fuck is under the hill? Why am I some kind of villain yet I'm supposed to stop him, me, whoever? Just, one time, in plain words, explain to me what exactly I'm meant to do and how I'm meant to do it."

"John the Younger, plain words do not suit you, but let me try. You are meant to stop the Elder from killing off the last of the old ones, namely we of the woods. When we are gone he will control, in a way, the space between worlds. He will have dominion over the periphery. This will not be good for the world at large. The veil between our perceptions, our universes, must stay intact until the ones without sight are ready to watch the veil be rent."

"So, I'm to kill some guy in a factory or invisible evil animals become visible and the world falls to bits?"

"I would not word it so crudely, but yes, in essence your words are mostly true."

"Great. So, let's get on with it. Let's march into that joint, metaphorical guns blazing, burn it to cinder. Then we head back here, grab a brandy and relax. Sure, this is easy. Nothing quite so invigorating in the morning than murdering a theoretical father figure on a hill. Wonderful."

"John, I believe you need to see him again. His words may be an easier pill to swallow."

"Who?"

"Hephaestus, who else would have the knowledge necessary?"

"He's dead… here. You want us to go back to the other place, don't you?"

"Yes, and this time you will not run."

He sighs deeply, "Fine. But give me till tomorrow. I need to exist in a real world for a bit. I need solidity."

"Fine. Good luck. We shall leave at noon."

"Until then…"

## 64. Rediscoveries.

John remembers his life as a linear motion bisected by his arrival at the office. He holds himself, shivering, in the great bed now left to disuse. The walls crawl with discreet alphabets, ink running from the ceiling, bleeding out mutant phrases into existence. The cold sweat upon his brow, now blackened with imagined ink, begins to fall upon the starched and dusty sheets. He reads from the imagined ledger. He watches his ink-sweat phrases upon the bed. He studies the bleeding pages soaking through the walls. He whispers their meanings, in voices of distant mimicry.

> *"John my boy! Thank the gods of old and new that you found this missive! I was worried to death (Ha!) that this would not be found!"*

Hephaestus' handwriting is rising up from the book, floating inches from John's eyes. The pages sit, still holding tight to the old words from when things were more linear.

> *"Please know that I did not mean to deceive you with the words previously read on these pages. They are wisdom. They led you to the point where these can be read. You should know by now that the Elder, the demon, is a shadow of yourself. You should know by now that there is another place to go, a true world of physical reality where we may all sit again if the further works of this*

*esteemed locality are good.*

*Now, John, I do not expect you to seal the rift; stop the villain; cure yourself; and become as I was, all at once. For now you must use everything the office and its staff have taught you to fulfill your part of the coming days. Succinctly put: please end that shadow on the hill. Drive it to the other place with the light of your vision. The healing will begin there. You will become whole again. You will feel yourself growing again as once you felt before your first death on that cursed place (bless the name of your brother). Then, and only then can you begin the true work of this place. Be the man I was, and the man I previously believed myself to be.*

*Salvation is yours to deliver if you can muster the strength. I will see you again soon. Or at least someone so very much like me, I use the same term for him for expediency.*

*Bless you John the Younger and take care of Kali and the boy. He will soon grow into something you've never before seen... wait for it, trust me. Walk with love my friend.*

*-Hephaestus, from one room over.*

John watches as the letters float away, turning to mist as they reach the ceiling. He stares blankly at the book, its letters re-chained to their paper master. He places the book back down, noticing the key sitting in the spot he left it those long weeks ago.

"Hello, key? Any messages for me? Location for your lock? Air-born writing? Anything?"

He shakes the key to no avail. Frustrated he shoves it into his pocket.

"I need a brandy."

## 65. The Hierophant, desperate for a drink, spins itself.

He walked with an internal conviction. His life was shifting again; his thoughts were weighted with Maggie, heavy on the prospect of being employed and being alone. He walked for what seemed like miles to the spot where the neighborhood pub once libated the masses, gone these long years.

John approached the door and with an effort popped it from its rust laden hinges. The dust rose and the skeletal remains of shelving and chairs sat there, lonely, dry. He walked on the door, and said hello to the local barmen, gone these long years.

"Beer and a shot of well whiskey please," John sat, and ruminated on the ghost of his beer. "I didn't know this place reopened."

He waved his hands in dirty air, nodding in recognition.

"Just making conversation I suppose. Sounds good to me… but tomorrow. For now, I think I will drink, feel sorry for myself. Let's see how the light effects my eyes in the morning. Cheers."

He sipped from the air, and saw the faces of demons. He grew discontent. He paid and left. The bills disturbed the dust. He coughed on the dust swirling about his head. The bar creaked; he sighed and walked into the air, and stopped, "Hephaestus?"

"John the Younger, I hope upon hope that no alcohol has touched your lips this day," John heard the air say.

He mumbled to himself then, and let his arm be lead back into the dark interior. He removed the dirty tablecloth from a table near the back of the pub, and sat. And there he laughed, and worried; there he mimed drink and song, revelry and discovery. After hours of inhaling dust, he stumbled out into the cold night, revived by the conversation.

Somewhere Hephaestus was laughing.

Somewhere the boundaries were thinning.

In the streets a man sang and danced until he found what he sought, a parlay with an old friend.

The singing man can vaguely recall the sound of broken glass, and the dull throb of screams from a place unseen.

## 66. Busted, cold busted.

John walks with a heavy head. His world is split between belief and logic, science and the coming night. When he closes his eyes, the horrific pictures from the television and papers flash in the darkness.

He sees his hands covered in blood, remembering the laughter choking in his throat.

He thinks himself insane.

He mutters in a futile attempt to put to order the garbled mass of sequence-less moments and conversations which sit where his past should be.

Moving with the pace of worry, he tries to make linear the chaos of his life after the fall.

"Let's get this straight, shall we? We shall. I know I am John. I remember most of my childhood, through the night on the hill, then some blanks, high school, a short stink in the hospital, a bit of college, Maggie, then that stupid ad… that's where it gets weird. So I meet with the girl, the kid, and the fat man, some trees, hairless things, and philosophy. OK, I can almost take that. Sure, it's a weird tree. I'm an open kind of guy. I can take that. We all did a little acid now and then, a flashback, nothing more. It's a weird place… or, I found an office that opened a door to a new reality as seen through the sides of my eyes, and now I'm an unknowing messiah that is supposed to kill himself. But not kill him as self. I, he, is to kill an older, other self, and thus save the world. Christ, it seemed real enough as I was experiencing it. I mean, we did speak to the little trees. The Child is there. I should go back. I should ride this thing out and see what happens. I mean, if it is true than I've done the world some good… if it's not true I hang out with a couple of strange people in a nice house. No harm there. Hell, even Maggie gets a nice house out of this… why does Maggie seem like Kali to me? Why…"

His monologue is interrupted by the flashing lights and accompanying siren typical of the moment before your life is about to be permanently changed.

Sirens whoop.

"Ah, hello Constable."

"Hello," his voice is stressed. His mind is dancing with ideas of cults and conspiracies. "You are one Mr. John Weishaupt, correct?"

"Yes. I am indeed one Mr. John Weishaupt. And you are?"

"I am Constable Aaron Seidel. You've met my partner, Detective Wilson."

"Oh, indeed! It is nice to make your acquaintance Constable Seidel!"

"Yeah, nice. Hands above your head John. Now, I'm going to approach you real slow. Please stay still. No one will hurt you."

"It's fine. I'm just taking a stroll, not on some murderous rampage."

"Not funny. People are missing. Strangely enough all of them with ties to you and that organization you folks run out on the logging roads."

John is surprised that the handcuffs do not hurt as much as the movies let on. He sits quietly ruminating over the painless cuffs as the car moves steadily to the station. The Police Officer is giving a soliloquy to John. The Police Officer's tone is gloating, is celebratory as John stops listening, deciding to watch as the lights move by the window. He plays a game, one learned in long car rides of his youth. In the game he follows a single ray of light on the windshield as he moves beneath. As the car passes beneath the source the light propels the car forward, like the poles of an unseen boatman.

He awakes from his revelry confined in a large cell, head aching. Smells like a hospital, he thinks, squinting at the sterile white walls.

"John. We saw the basement. We know what happened. Come clean, it'll be easier on you."

"Where am I?"

John has no idea as to his locality. The notions of fog at the edges of his awareness clear as the walls and iconic bars give him bearing.

"Jail? I was just walking to Maggie's a second ago."

"Don't pull that crap with me now. You're in county lock up; your name is John Weishaupt; you've been talking to me for over an hour; you are here because we have reasons to link you to the death of Mr. Cassiel Landry and the disappearance of one Hephaestus James Bonobus."

John sits on the hard metal bench, the cold of its surface bleeding into his hands. He watches the policeman give his speech as waves of nausea and confusion beat upon him.

"Now… as I was saying, the evidence is all over the basement. We have hair, partial fingerprints, and numerous statements, which place you down there. Can you explain that, sir?"

"What the hell is this? Where is The Child? Where is Kali?"

"Sir, John, they have been notified as per your request. Now, please stop jerking me around and tell me how it is that you have no knowledge of Cassiel Landry's probable murder, yet we find evidence that you were at the scene?"

"Cass is dead? But, he was missing. Your friend came to my office and asked if I knew where he went; I said no. Are you sure it's him? What evidence? What the hell is going on here?"

"Christ... look, I'm going to go get you some water, and we'll start this thing from the beginning. Will that be OK?"

"Yeah, that's... that's fine. But please come back with reports contrary to what I've heard, or, in their stead a full and detailed account of what you've supposedly conversed with me about."

"Yes. I'll do just that. Be right back, try and keep awake."

The gentleman in the blue jacket leaves the cell, swinging it closed in his wake. John looks into the other place, and the walls shimmer and squirm. John places himself in a dungeon beneath the hill. He sees the movements of his evil other in this farce. He paces and tries to conjure some way to return to the office in the woods. He draws, with his finger, a door, and it fails to appear. He tries, as he has done before, to pull back the veil separating the worlds, to control this place... and so he fails.

"Bonobus... I could really use a hand here. These people intend to kill me, to burn our trees. I could seriously use an assist on this one."

The Officer approaches the door, somber faced, a pitcher of water in one hand, a key in the other. OK, John, let's start this thing over again. He turns the key in the ancient looking lock. John glows as his vision grows pure again. The Officer slumps forward into John's cell, revealing behind him a small child and a smiling woman, pipe in hand. Sometimes wishes are granted through well-placed strikes.

"Oh John, you were missed! Let us leave this den of villainy and return home. I believe our appointment at the hill is nigh."

"I thought we were under the hill? This place stinks of the Elder."

The Child's voice, like gravity, like the movement of glaciers, "No, Younger one, this place is a reflection of the laws of the world which we cannot abide by. We should make a hasty exit before the constable returns to us."

"You speak with wisdom, Child."

They step gingerly over the still, uniformed, body on the way to the exit.

"They sleep for now, Younger. Please do not dally about in these places."

John stops to turn back, to take in the victory. His footsteps tinted with blood, a singular line leading to salvation.

"Come John, this place will be angry in the coming moments."

The three walk out, hand in hand, into the welcoming night; stars shimmer their approval; sirens of a distant place, echoing faintly upon sweetened air.

## 67. The evidence of fault lines.

An Earthquake in a small town. An unfamiliar omen shifting the houses built upon the previously motionless granite.

An earthquake in a small town, trees fall, graves are uncovered in the uprooted soil.

In an ancient manor in a medium-growth wood, a man is sitting on a bed, shaking from sub-strata and anxiety. The shaking man, John, is rocking in a cold sweat. In a motion, slightly forced by tectonic motion, he reaches out to one of the books left over from the reign of the one before him. He reads from the book given to him from an elder long gone. On a random page he feels the pull of something from the other place. He reads a section at, what he would have previously believed to be, random:

> *We teach you about the dogs/birds first because they are the most evident, the closest to existing in this world. This is part of the lessons of the Masters now long gone, long returned to the other place. They are variables, placeholders in the mathematics of the world as ascertained by the ones who will write this book. Once those placeholders are easily ignored, the truth of vision will be allowed. This is what the other place was, and will be like. This is what a merging of the variances of sight would produce, and once did. This is the goal.*

In its darker recesses, John's mind is failing him. His world, or worlds, have collapsed, leaving behind black holes, spiraling around his losses. He wakes to new rooms previously unnoticed. In his mind, he is achieving a perfect sight, the completeness of the periphery.

In the eyes of The Child and the waif he sees death, a dark tapestry in place of recognition.

He remembers digging the holes where trees once rooted.

He sees himself as a monster, a machine built to murder birds and people with his horrific powers.

In the darker recesses, John's mind begins to hatch plans and scheme schemes. He will follow the path set before him by the giant in the wool suit. He will burn to cinders anything not following the new ways. “The Burned-Over District” will flourish again, whether by fire or growth it will be determined by his motions through the coming days.

In the darker recesses John's mind is unhinged, seeing in parallel, seeing as schism. He has taken on all aspects of the periphery, probably too soon. The balance of vision is uneven, weighted in some bizarre ratio leaving the mind barren, screaming, and mostly serene.

John is sitting in a room he does not recognize.

John is praying to himself in the words of the office.

He is sitting, chanting the words as given to him by Hephaestus and the office alike.

Blank.

He looks forward.

The walls crawl in translucent arcs and waves, vines moving, the breathing of the office mimicking his own. It expresses its influence.

The youngest of the house sits near a rotting tree.

The youngest of the house sits thoughtless and alone,

unmotivated by presence to make life.

The woman in the basement shivers, then glows. Grinning, she holds herself in preparation for the dusk.

He is blank.

He is shifting from light to dark, from gray to sepia, from existence to the void. The house whispers in his ear, or so it is perceived. Muttering, he holds the arms of the chair and digs his nails into the artificial wood.

He whispers:

"In the yard, a little boy stands with his balloons. A man stands in confusion. A woman with child's eyes watches over them with compassion.

"The child body smiles and waves a free hand. Policy is harmony through intelligence and proper awareness… this ever more dangerous world.

"Please obey all written and verbal commands… terminated. The boy shall not be bothered. Do not touch the balloons… a primary company directive. The female form yelps, Oh, I miss seeing him like this!"

His fingers dig deeper in, the nails begin to crack and splinter; the beginnings of a deluge forms in the spaces between. He whispers:

"Kali hugs John from the side… The Child runs to John's other… He holds his hand… They smile. The walls run forever through me, the outside place is false, is not real.

"We are home here and the blood and spatter are fitting baptism… The child hands a balloon and nods to The Tree. John releases the balloon, into The Tree, and he looks back down from it. As they speak the house shifts on its foundation. It knows the importance of the scene being played out within itself. The house knows of the schism in both of them, it knows of the growing wants of reprieve from weight carried for too long.

“A glimpse of movement from the branch, and he searches upward, seeing nothing.

“He stands, placing his hand upon the wall, searching for a signal from within. He spins to face the fading bed, the bookshelf full of carrion.

“Goodbye my dearest. She lifts up on toes and kisses John on the cheek. Oh god The Tree. The Tree is almost finished. The Tree beckons to Hephaestus to join him again. The pulsing of the ground is exponential. The Trees feel the change approaching. His new eyes had yet to take in the stars. His new eyes are here, taking this in…”

The sounds of the Victrola seeping through the walls wake him from his delirium. He smells upon the air the waft of tea, brewed from the remaining fruits of the sacred Tree. He feels himself warm over as the curious comforts of the house soak into him.

His voice like a reed in light breeze, "This cycle is bound to the universe with diaphanous materials, and is set to fall to pieces in the coming days. Soon we will dance again upon the shores of that better place, with softer sight and lighter hearts. The sirens of this world will cease; the dogs will quiet; the periphery will lay back down upon us, a comforting blanket from a long missing mother. I will make this end. The man on the hill will bring forth, for good or ill, an end to this."

He leaves that place of whispers, and reenters the life of the house. Kali sits at her desk drawing spirals on paper, radiating at seeing John's reappearance.

"Kali! I had the most wonderful dream. The words of the universes streaking through simultaneous visions! The walls bled and the sirens wailed in cacophonous music, showing me where the finale will happen! Where is The Child? We need to go."

“John the Younger, I could not be more pleased. I never once doubted that you would impart the values that will cause the wave to collapse!"

"Thank you, my dearest Kali. Now, where is our Child? Things are moving at a speed best suited to his youthful exuberance."

"Where else could he be? In the yard, tending to the rotting one."

"Good. I will need you to watch this place. We are going back. I know now what needs to be done."

"Be careful, my love. I expect you home and in possession of all your pieces and bits."

"Indeed. Until the next."

## 68. We both know the way this time.

In the yard, The Child sits in full lotus under the sickly tree. He is as still as statuary. As John approaches, he is jolted back to life. The Child, rising like a marionette on tangled strings, eyes unfocused, looks drained of life, pallid. John watches this macabre dance as he crosses the browned and patchy grass. The Child grows firmer in the dirt, his eyes gain footing.

"Hail Tree Keeper!"

"Hello, John.”

"How goes your righteous duty this day?"

"I sit under a tree."

"Are you feeling correct? You don't seem yourself."

"We traveled to that other place. I left my guard. And now you are lost. You have forgotten all that he taught you. I sit under a tree, dying."

"I am sorry that I ran. I had doubts. I know what must be done now. And if you will accompany me, I would like to go back and finish this thing."

The Child approximates a smile, it sits distorted on his face, "I am glad for this John. Now, let us get prepared. A few things must be done before we set off on this monotonous repetition of a journey."

## 69. A time of games.

It was autumn and they were young. John and Tyler had escaped the confines of the block, moved quickly through the secret paths known only to children. They had invented a game earlier that season. They had invented a game in which one would run, the other chase and call out the names of the things which they were not.

"I'll get you now! Airplane.... Tree... Car... Villain... Runner!"

The game had moved from the stream of the neighborhood to the forested hills rolling to the east. It was when Tyler was a tree that he was finished, caught, and held to the final judgment of youth, being 'it'. They now ran through paths between razor shrubs and rusting trees.

"Bicycle... Soldier... Parent... Boss... Ollie Ollie... I'll get you monster."

The game had John run through the covert space in the fence upon the hill. John and Tyler ran full speed in the now abandoned spaces between buildings and the piles of industry left to oxidize. The wind picked up, and the words fell short of intended ears. The wind picked up and John pressed forward against the onslaught. He heard the screams from behind him, the nouns and occupations for what he was not. The game ran them joyfully through the meandering circuits of nothing much to do.

"Pancake... Woodsman... Calliope..."

The sound was small at first, a snap of a branch, cold in fall breeze. The sound rumbled louder as the pile gave way under Tyler. The snap of human branches, amplified by the moving echo chamber, as he was twisted to ruin upon that hill of rust and powder.

"Tyler?"

John's eyes welled up with tears as he looked into a pile of flesh and concrete stained with what was previously his playmate, his brother.

"Tyler? Tyler? Ty…?"

The sound of branches and screams had stopped. His eyes had turned to water. All that was left of the cacophony was the swaying of branches, the crumbling concrete, and the sobbing of a child now holding his knees atop the ruins. His brother broken amid the rumble, he hears the sound of cracking again. He sits and weeps as the wind pays no testament to his loss.

## 70. The patron Saints of incidental regrets.

"It seems every time I look around a new facet appears, a new hum in the cosmos," The Child in the Yard's voice echoes. "It seems every time I look around some old thing reappears. We're never rid of the past, it seems."

It seems to John that he is not speaking at all, more so a form of internal mechanism, the vibrations of sleep.

"What kind of old things do you see returning?"

"Oh, you know, old friends, ancient trees, a familiar turn of phrase. We walk to see the outline of Hephaestus once more. It's all old things, memories made real."

"I see. Well, soon it will end, I suppose. Soon we put an end to the story of the Elder."

"Indeed. He will feed the Trees soon enough. Look at the sky, Young Master John. Do you see the split?"

"Of course."

"The sky was not always this way. Once, it was united. Once the sky was perfect and blue with no signs of the tearing that now disfigures it. But we tried to see too early, we forced our hand, and this place went to ruin. The eldest ran to their places, and we took dominion over ours. But, now, as the years of ruin progress, we find the darkness building up again, and becoming more evident. We are in the position to close the rift, if it allows us to. John, we have a chance to make right a problem far older than that of your Elder who lives too long in your memory and your name. "

"I understand the need. However, the details seem hazy. What, exactly, happened to cause the worlds to split; the sky to rend; and to being this place to ruin?"

The Child gestures to the landscape now growing wild with ancient marble and broken glass, "A thing, a prior form of whom you called Hephaestus, caused this."

"Hephaestus? How could he? He would never do something like this."

"He, or one very much like him, had no idea that this would happen. He found a way to bring both worlds into equality; to balance this place with ours. The idea was… flawed. Both places were ruined. This place of ruins, and our place of offices and make believe, were thrown into a balance more prone to unrest than peace. He has, since then, sought to make right this mistake, to take into his employ the one to fix this. He has spent the long years searching for himself in new clothes. He has spent these long years searching for a new partner to replace the undying on the hill. He believed that could be you. Blessed are the names of the fallen."

"How long has he known about me?"

"Well, not long… and forever. He, and the ones before him, had an awareness of something on the horizon. I suppose he knew about you when you took up your search. The real question is, when did you know about him?"

"Well, Cassiel, at the shop I found your address in called him the fat man. I guess that's when."

"You know better than that."

"But, that's how it happened."

"Come now John, you can't be that stupid. Look around you. You know you invented the fat man as a substitute for your lost father. You've used him as proxy to all your longings. He fills the void left by your family and by your brother. That is why you forced Cassiel to give you that book, if there was a book. That was right before you needlessly slaughtered him, of course.

"No. He was a friend, why do you say these terrible things?"

"Because you've invented the whole thing, John. The split is in you, not the sky. None of this is real. Turn back."

"But..."

"Turn back!"

John awakes in the office, his brow coated in sweat. He looks desperately for The Child, the path, the rent sky. Finding no mental purchase, no objects familiar to the moment before, he realizes he was in a dream.

John sits in the bed and holds his knees. He rocks himself in an attempt to regain a measure of comfort. The voice of his dreams still echo through the room. His voice is whispers, unknowable. Sitting there, still, meditating on the visions of his sleep, he debates reality. In the burgeoning dawn, he doubts the veracity of his own narrative. He doubts his visions as seen through the twin proxies of awareness and understanding.

# 71. Road trip.

The morning wakes them, those of the house. The morning finds him, the newest, soaked and ragged, awake from a night spent in anguishing dreams. The Child stares at his walls, waiting for the work to begin. Kali is below, weeping for Maggie now lost in the margins of The Treeless house and direction-less doors.

Gathered in the library, now coated in dust, cobwebbed and molded, they sit awaiting words. The Child sits like Buddha on the floor as Kali stands before him, looking down into his lifeless eyes. They breathe out in unison as John enters. Motes of dust dance in spirals.

The dance has begun: the players in their place; the setting set. John walks and takes his place next to Kali. With a slow, purposeful movement, The Child's head turns toward John.

The child breaks the silence.

"John," he turns back to Kali with horrific slowness, "Kali, we gather here to give our farewell to this place, for some time at least. Our journey will be long by some, and short as shadows for others."

"Child," Kali's voice is glacial, practiced, "we know what today entails. We know the task ahead is important. I wish you both good blessings. I shall remain to the last, sole holder of the office in the woods."

"Thank you Kali, well said. John, you are better prepared this time?"

"I am, Child of the Yard," John lies.

He has not spoken lies since his arrival at the firm. The dream of the night before rattles him. It gives him pause, doubt over the coming trials, the coming days of complete belief necessary to exist in that place.

"Your eyes seem wrong, John the Younger. We can delay for one more day if that suits you better."

"No. We go today. It needs to be today. Kali, please watch over this place. You are all that's left of us now."

"I will my dear. Please, return to me as soon as math allows."

"Let us go," The Child rises. John is shocked at his newly acquired height, now broaching his shoulders.

"Indeed," A dead friend waits.

In the woods, they walk with disinterest. In the woods, John speaks with languor. His spirit is dissolved. In the woods, the ennui is palpable. In the woods, he walks with The Child out of a perverted notion of loyalty to the ideas made sacred by a freshly lost father. He is part of this battle, real or fictitious. He will be the redeemer, even if it takes what is left of him to do so.

## 72. This seems familiar.

The path is easier this time.

The path soon hypnotizes them into believing that they travel faster than relativity should allow.

The sky soon tears itself in that now familiar manner.

The path winds its way through "The Burned-Over District," through the ruins of the land which came before, and finally, into the shadow of the office. The shadow shifting as mirage in the gloaming.

They walk in silence, The Child radiating with annoyance at John's flight.

John walks with abandon of what came before.

John forgets himself again, and lets in the idea of being a redeemer, of being something truly unique in the world.

He lets go of his past, of his doubt.

As he moves forward, the threads connecting him to his previous self are severed. The parts that made him the man who walked down a dusty road in an ill-fitted suit are getting weaker. The threads of memory connecting him to a forgotten father and dead brother are failing upon each step.

They arrive at the footprint of the office, in time to see the sun blank out behind the rift. He looks into the sky and sees the tear turn a shade of purple as it swallows the sun. The Child stands at his right, unmoving and cold.

"It eats the sun."

"It masks it from us for moments, no more, no less. In this moment we are closest to that other place, the one which seemed your home those long years."

"I can feel that. Let's go inside and find Hephaestus."

"No. You cannot see inside there. We will wait here. He will join us soon enough."

"And why can I not go in?"

"Because you are not ready to see it. In there the truth is pure, unfiltered. In there the metaphors pull no punches."

"I'm tired of this, Child. I'm going in. If I'm to be your savior, the bringer of a new era I think I can handle anything the mirror of my home can throw at me."

"No. You may not enter."

"That is where you are wrong, Child. I am your boss, am I not?"

"This is true, and you know it."

"Good, then I enter. You may follow or you may remain here."

"I will wait for you, John the Younger," The Child's voice heavy with disdain, "but be warned that what you see in there may not serve you well."

"Child. I will go in, and whatever is in there will serve me as it sees fit. I am the master of this place, at least it's mirror, and so I enter as is my whim."

"You sound like the other one. Now go. Find out what exists in the shadows."

"Indeed, I will. Please be here when I return."

John approaches the office, now taking the shape of a roman villa, roofless, broken. It sits in this place with stonewalls crawling with ivy and moss. It sits with large gouges taken from the walls.

As perceived, the office sits with the same energy and life in this place as it does in the one he calls home. Entering through what was the kitchen, now a leaf shaped gash in the rock, he strains to see any sign of occupation, any signal that this place holds some of the powers of his own. He sees movements in the shadows and knows that this is part of him, of home.

"Hello, office."

The walls swell out in displeasure. The house sighs and sways in disbelief that he would reenter, especially in his current state. John feels this disquiet and tries, with both sides of his sight, to calm the energies now swirling in his midst. The energy feels like himself, or caused by himself. It is familiar on a primal level, this sylvan enclave. It feels like the spirit of the true place as seen through a new filter, reincarnation through perception and meandering walks.

"House. I am John the Younger, a visitor from the other place. In that place I am manager here. I bring good tidings and no ill will. Please find me dissimilar to one who once betrayed this place and bears a similar name."

The house settles and tries, in the subtle ways of architecture, to pulse its acceptance of this new visitor.

"Is anyone home?" He raises his voice slightly, feeling an unexpected trepidation at entering what is, ostensibly, his home, "Kali? Hephaestus? Dura? What lives here now?"

From the basement a voice issues, and begs his entry. It is familiar enough, yet John cannot place where he has heard it before.

"Hephaestus? Is that you?"

He descends a spiral stairway of algae covered marble. The air grows thick with each step. The sounds of writhing and whispers grow as John's head passes the line of the above world, into the one below. As he steps to the ground level he sees, through the greenhouse mist, outlines of people and hears their faint whispers.

They are gathered in three. They are gathered in the shape of a triangle.

He knows this as the mirror image of the study in the office.

He knows this as a mirror of a meeting which has happened, and happened again, across long stretches of time.

"Hello, John," that same voice carries across the mist. "Please, be our guest at this, our first meeting of many." His shadow arm gestures down to a stone bench, inlaid with angels and the sketches of plants. "Have a seat, we have much to discuss."

It was with that utterance John knew the voice. It was his father's, or, at the least, a fair mimic.

"Dad?"

"No, John, far from. I was called John of the hill."

"The Elder," John spits with its utterance. He hisses at an older version of himself.

"No, John my boy. This is John as I knew him," Hephaestus, looking twenty years younger, thin, virile, steps out from the darkness. Hephaestus' face reminds John of The Child's.

"We are in the other place, as well you know. This is an echo of what came before; as I am an echo of a previous self. Hold no malice sprung from the other place here."

"Hephaestus? It is good to see you looking so well. How is this not the enemy? He's me!"

"John," the mellifluous voice of Kali calls out, "this is the way of things here. You should not have come."

John looks to her and sees Dura, old, broken, "What is this?"

"John. Know that this is not what it seems," the desiccated corpse of a child lays supine, decayed, yet still recognizable. The Child lays in perfect stillness, his mouth the only movement.

"Oh god, Child!" John moves towards the rotting, but is stopped by the elder vision of himself.

"This place is not for you. Go outside and wait. You will be met by one of us in our own time. It is good to see me again, so young and unsoiled by memory and the things we've done to harm those around us."

He runs, vaulting up two steps at a time. He runs, knocking down ancient masonry until he falls upon the yard, panting. The Child places his hand on John's shoulder in comfort.

"No! You can't be here, and there. Why are you here and there?"

"I told you no good would come from that place. You cannot see it for how it truly exists… only that bent shadow. That is the fissure made flesh. What did you see?"

"You don't want to know."

"Yes. I do. I would not have asked otherwise. Please detail me on your trip inside."

"I saw Hephaestus… and Kali, but she was Dura… and the Elder, but not the Elder… it was like a dream."

"What else?"

John looks to The Child and wonders how much he knows about what he has seen. John wonders if he knows what lies in the basement.

"You."

"I assumed as much. And I was, let us say, less than healthy?"

"Yes. You were dead, laying upon a couch."

"I can see how that would be disturbing to you. That was not me, John the Younger."

"Then who? It did bear a striking resemblance to you."

"It was a player in this game long lost. He will return now that I find myself steadily growing older. Those are echoes, memories made tangible by your presence here."

John looks upon the boy, and sees the same light in his eyes as were in Hephaestus'. He sees the boy, now more than ever, as a placeholder in the movements of the periphery. He sees the boy as no longer stalled, a fluid thing moving through time and space again, unlike that stilled and rotting mimic in the basement.

"The pairings I've heard spoken of, he was yours?"

"No. He was more a brother in a journey that was never taken. What lies beneath is a manifestation of a wrong. A wrong wrought upon the world when a mistake was made so many years ago. What lies beneath us is me, but not me. It is what I have become since your arrival, aging, dying. You've killed us all, John the Younger."

The child looks to the earth, depressed.

"No… God no… I didn't mean you any harm. I was lost and needed a place to belong. Who knew it would come to this?"

The Child begins to answer but is interrupted by the swinging open of a door.

"Gentlemen," the young Hephaestus walks from the doorway leading into the villa. He is alone and smiling, a cigar waving in his fist. "I am glad you have once again returned. I take it that young master John has had a change of heart? Well, no matter, we are all here now."

"Quite. It's good to lay mortal eyes upon you again, my old

friend," The Child seems uplifted by the company. "John here has had me down in spirits since the news of your co-conspirators in the basement."

"Yes. We feared you would hear. So it goes. Now, on to business. John, what brings you back after such a frightful departure last you walked this space?"

"I have realized the unevenness of this all. My head swam, and when I awoke I knew that I was the only one available to make progress in this world and in my own. I realize that I want equilibrium. I know that I have harmed you all in some way by my arrival. I started a chain reaction that has cascaded down to all of us, burying us. And the one on the hill laughing through it all. I will have caused the rift to spread further with little hope for closure. I want that thing under the hill to end, and I think that you can help me with that… though, your choice of company of late leaves that in doubt."

"John, you should know that what is in the house is not the creature you know. This is all a simulacrum of something bigger. We are playing the roles as written for the time that this play goes on. If you stop the thing under the hill you may find your equilibrium. But, what lives here, lives here forever… until it does not. We all return, back and forth, the unbroken circle."

"I don't understand quite yet. This place isn't changed when something in ours changes? I thought this was like a mirror of ours, laid over our own."

"You have it nearly right. This place is unique while having qualities of the other. It is both mirror and metaphor. That is not important though. You have work to do."

"Yes. Work. So, quickly, how do I stop him?"

John's face is confident and strong in the yellow light of near dark. Hephaestus glows with pride, his de facto son rising to occasion. The Child stands, looking sickly to the men.

The Child speaks without inflection, "It is easy enough. You take his Tree."

Hephaestus walks to the side of the house, disappearing around the corner.

John looks to The Child.

The Child stares forward, unmoving in an eerie echo of the basement.

The giant, with massive, springing steps, returns again, holding a small ax.

"Take this and plant it where you may. Take his Tree and the rest will fall. Take back the hill and reclaim what was lost. Then we may be on the road to finding the way home."

John takes the ax from Hephaestus. He feels no power in the thing, no special magic. It is, quite simply, an ax.

"So, I find his Tree, and chop it down… with this?"

"It will be an effective way of stopping the onslaught of what has held on for too long."

"And what of permission from the Birds?"

"The Birds? No permission needed… they don't exist. They are place holders, metaphors used to show you an operant principle which you cannot understand with your current model of reality. Everything you've seen is metaphor for something more intrinsic to yourself. This world, and the other, in a very real way, are you."

"So, they don't exist?"

"In a way, yes. But, as far as permission is concerned, consider your permission granted," Hephaestus smiles and pats him on his shoulder.

"So, what is here are archetypes of the things and people I know. This place is metaphor taken to a physical level. To see truth is to find that sliver between both places. Between periphery and what I call my world. This is correct?"

"Indeed. Correct enough to continue on your path."

"Thank you, Hephaestus. The Child and I will go back and try to end this thing once and for all. I hope that you return to us soon. Goodbye, my dear manager."

"Indeed. Goodbye, master John, and master Keeper."

## 73. Hey, you guys had a party while I was gone.

In a very real way, Kali and Maggie are dead.

They ceased to be when a ritual was undertaken, a substance imbibed, a contact made.

In another equally real way, they thrive in their respective offices; they are a happy house of philosophers and misfits.

In yet another way John will only see Kali from now on, as her duty sits her in the path of the office; as Maggie's duty sits her in the path of the place of doors, an office in need of repair.

As Maggie is in that place, she ceases to perform the functions of the girl whom John knew, happy and sated in the shared fallen graces of approaching 30.

In the ways of the periphery, all of this is true, and quite literally a lie.

John and The Child stride confidently from the woods, chattering in low voices. The yard greets them, brown, dead. The Tree is slumped over, tumorous in its animal form, rotted in its vegetable state.

The Child and the man stop and look at the sickened yard, their shoulders and heads slumping down in despair. Time, he thinks, is running short for this Tree. Time is running short for this iteration of the periphery and the people held therein.

John's thoughts run from Tree to house, to Maggie to Kali, to Hephaestus and the others who were lost to time and the long knives of a mind gone too far.

His fractured awareness moves from visions of blood and dying trees to flashing sunlight through the forest ceiling.

In tightening circles, he moves around the yard.

With each circuit, he moves ever closer towards the house.

A ghostly image of a child, and a transparency of a heavy man float through the scene as the circles of walking coincide with the entry of the office.

The house warms in welcome to the conquering heroes freshly returned from the land of ruins and desolation.

"Keeper of The Tree, John the Younger, welcome returns!" Kali's face glows as she grasps them into unbalance in her enthusiastic embrace.

John stands with straightened back, military like. The Child slightly as he mimics his stance.

"Hello Kali, greetings from that other place."

"Things went better in the other place this time, I assume?"

"Yes. I believe we know how to end this charade."

"Oh, how fun! How do we stop the things which squirm under the hill?"

"Well, I think I take this ax which Hephaestus gave me and…"

"What! You saw him again! Oh joy of joys, you must tell me how this happened!"

"In time you will know all. He told me to cut down the Elder's Tree, and this ends. I have reservations about ending the life of a Tree, but it must be done."

"Well, that sounds grand. One question, if I may… how do we find his Tree?"

"A fine question… well, I assume we walk to the hill and look around. Find what perverted version of a Tree he keeps there, and turn it to kindling."

The child speaks as law, "That may be slightly more complicated this time around, John. The Elder has placed wards up since your last visit. We will have to fight our way in. Perception of that place is the only way to enter."

"Of course he would. It couldn't possibly be that easy. But, we must try. Honor the memories of Dura and Gideon, and the countless Trees which dried and burnt in his name." John speaks as mimicry. His words sing in the tone of Hephaestus.

"So, when do we make our assault on the enemy?" Kali asks in a mildly amused tone. "When do we lay siege on the castle?"

"Tomorrow. Tomorrow it all ends," in John's voice can be heard a tremble, a quiver of recognition that this is all madness. "Tomorrow we take his Tree. Now, have we heard from our friend in the Place of Doors and Vortices?"

# 74. The Emperor(reversed).

Let us pretend, together, that in a derelict factory on a nameless hill there sits something evil, something leftover from a more savage time.

Let us take a second to think about a man, tall and thin, striking horrific poses over piles of dust and rusted metal.

If we were to pretend, just hard enough, we would see this as John the Elder, the maniac aspect of the periphery, a remnant of the previous generation; the one of Dura and Gideon; of Hephaestus; of The Child wearing his adult outfit.

He, while on the hill, paces and mumbles, waving his arms in the air to solidify his point.

He filibusters for hours on end, staring out at the valley floors, the place of an office he calls his home.

He plans to kill the inhabitants of that place.

He plans to leave himself alone in this universe, the sole holder of an arcane gnosis, a hidden secret way to see the other universes.

He plans the murder of all things that came after him, and by that strange reversible aspect of this place, before.

He stands and screams out the locations where he will bury those that feed The Tree in the woods.

He salivates as he dreams of watching the reptile Tree fall to ruin.

He sits waiting for John's decision to join him in full, or be subsumed in totality under the weight of his perception and his hatred.

In his mind:

He will be the truth of the two worlds.

He will teach a new generation of seers in his ways.

His eyes will be the device by which the universe observes itself, the pinnacle of all growth as perceived by these flawed machines.

He will control the growth and split of the periphery and the focused; of the minds and the bodies of who are to come.

He will take John up, and place him upon a hill.

He will upset the forces of balance and compromise.

He will raise in their stead a monument to premature action built with the wood of the once sacred Trees, now felled and replaced with a kind of chimerical cousin, both demon and angel, both destroyer and builder.

He will stride forth and create upon the universe a pattern marked by chaos and ignorance.

“Now I am become Death, the destroyer of worlds.”

## 75. Seekers of a more comfortable truth.

In the office.

In the office, in the woods.

In the house.

In the house that is the office.

In that place, which is the spiritual made physical.

In that place, where metaphor and action are inseparable, exists the remnants of the HJ Bonobus corp.

In that place John gesticulates wildly to the Trees.

In that place:

He screams for Maggie to call upon the god of that place to clear a way for her return.

He screams to John the Elder, the father who could not be.

He screams to Tyler, a brother left broken.

He screams to his unknown Mother, and to all the grotesque faces which have reached out for him in the fever dreams of his youth.

He spins in wild circles, frothing at the mouth.

And, then, as it appears to him, The Child walks across the yard.

“John. Your rain dance seems ineffective. The Tree is dead. The last of the fruit await picking.”

“Oh Child, you know the dance was always ineffective. I am simply waiting for the Elder to arrive so I can destroy him and end this whole disgusting epoch.”

“He will not come to you John the Younger. You must become proactive to end this war; for a war is how you have perceived it, as you have created it.”

“This was a battle waged before my arrival eldest young one. I am simply acting out the motions set forth by others to mimic the end of something which has never existed.”

“Yes. This is predetermined. But I believe you have overstated the amount. This world is your own, John. Do not forget that. You made me… and Maggie… and Kali, and the Elder, what we are. It is your job to end us as we currently sit. All things are, as you well know, transitory.”

“We are predetermined, yet our decisions matter. It's an aspect of his philosophy I've yet to grasp.”

“It's easy once you stop looking for an answer. This is a world of your creation, so if you want it to end, you end it. Kill yourself and the Elder dies. There is no difference between you and him. All this drama is the same matter expressing itself in different forms. You are the same being.”

“I am nothing like him.”

“John. You are HIM. He is your negative aspect. You are both the murderer and the Detective. There is no John the Elder. There is no John the Younger. There is only the observer and the point of observation.”

## 76. Illusory Maggie.

Maggie is not actually Maggie at this point. She exists as a placeholder for John to use as he sees fit. Maggie, to John, is his mother; is Kali; is the shadowy aspect of his old life. She's the one he left when his mind fractured one sweaty night in a horror show office building in a broken area of the world. Maggie, as far as a narrative can tell you is living in a Victorian house a few miles from a rotting tree. She is currently approaching a door, one of many.

She hums along to a tune that does not exist.

She walks down a corridor of doors, mostly useless, all without function save for a red handled affair, which was shown to her on a whimsical day in spring.

She is walking, somnambulating, towards the office in the woods. The sun is above her. The dirt is yet below her, differentiating her from the other, less lucky, followers of the Bonobus path.

Sirens chirp, waking her from her revelry.

"Please place your hands over your head and step off the side walk."

Maggie is terrified. She obliges the voice issued from the speaker atop the white and black Crown Victoria.

A person exits the car. He is dressed up as a Police Officer. The clasp on his gun is open. He holds silver bracelets on a chain.

"You are Kali Dee?"

“No, sir. My name is Maggie.”

Scribbling a note upon his small pad, he mutters back, “Yes, AKA Maggie, fine, great.”

“No AKA. I am Maggie. I have held this name since my birth. You should address me thusly. Kali exists in a differentiated body at the moment.”

“My mistake, I guess. I will make a note of this… 'differentiated body'.”

“What may I ask is this about?”

“Well, ma’am, I’m Detective Wilson. We’d like to discuss with you the incident which happened at the Ash Street Station.”

“I'm glad to answer all questions. What is the Ash Street Station?”

“The local police station ma’am, specifically the location where my colleague was bludgeoned into unconsciousness one week ago. We suspect it was done by Mister John Weishaupt and up to two accomplices, in an attempt to take evidence collected by Officer Seidel in regards to multiple missing persons cases.”

“Oh no! John would never do that! Just ask him. He's a good man, a fine manager.”

“Manager?”

“Yes. He is manager in both nominus and action at the esteemed Hephaestus James Bonobus Corp!”

“Of course, the place in the woods… Do you know where to find this John Weishaupt?”

“Of course I do. I was on my way there now. He lives in the office in the woods, the Hephaestus James Bonobus Corporation!”

“We’ve tried there numerous times since the incident. No answer. You're telling me he's there, now?”

"Yes. He is returned from the other place. He is John the Younger, bringer of balance!"

"Sure. Now we're going to take a little ride over there if you don't mind. I'd like a little chat with Mr. Weishaupt. I assume you don't mind giving me a nice reintroduction?"

"A pleasure, my darling Detective."

## 77. The ever spinning Chariot.

"...by blood or by certificate we are family now. Bound together in this our eternal struggle."

We join John mid-speech.

He is addressing the furniture in the front room, the place where once he innocently read nonsensical pamphlets while enjoying the snacks provided. Today he is giving a rousing address about the nature of the HJ Bonobus Corporation and the goings on there since his taking the mantle of leader.

Of course, the room is empty aside from him and a couch he calls Kali; but he is addressing his troops, his workers and compatriots in the ongoing battle against the perceived forces of the other side, of the periphery. A knock is issued from the front door, stopping his soliloquy just when he is about to enter the crescendo of the farce.

"What is this? A knock? Now? Now, of all times previous and to come, a knock is issued from the door to this very place? What form of temptation and villainy could possibly be interrupting such a grand meeting? Does he not know of the bell? Does he not know the umbrage we take at the sound of flesh on wood?"

From the other room John hears a gravel voice call out. "Master John, why not open the door and sate your questioning?"

"Ah, yes! Child, you're a wonder!"

John opens the door as fast as he can, the outside air rushing in to fill the vacuum. The Detective startles slightly back as Maggie twitches forward in a rare non-Newtonian motion of greeting.

"Maggie, my darling, what brings you from the place of doors with such poorly clad company?"

"You would not believe the stories this blue man has been spreading about you and the others in residence!"

"Mr. Weishaupt, may I come inside? I have some questions for you."

"You have poor timing. But I shall allow your entry this once, in deference to the young misses with whom you keep company. Be at peace here."

The Detective and Maggie enter the front hall. A fetid odor can be sensed, if the senses are prone to searching for such offense. He winces at the perceived stench. Maggie is unaffected.

"Good god." Detective Wilson steps backwards towards the door. He pulls out his gun, training it on John, simultaneously blocking Maggie with his other arm. He steps back and drags her along as he speaks, thinking he recognizes the unfortunate smell. "Stay where you are sir! What is that smell?"

The Detective knows the smell of a corpse. He knows he has found something foul.

John is smug in his dialogue, "I smell nothing, save for the faint waft of fruited incense from young Miss Kali's study. And may I further add, a bit of bad cologne coming from your direction."

Maggie is jubilant, giddy with John's insult. The Detective is considering his next move as Maggie pushes from him to stand in between John and the gun.

"Ma'am, I'm only here to protect, there's no need to escalate this situation. Please step away from him. We'll all have a nice talk outside while we wait for some of my friends to come along."

“That sounds nice. I would like a nice constitutional with the constabulary!”

“Yes John, that's a grand plan! Let us show him The Tree!”

“The Tree?”

He does not like the sound of 'The Tree'.

“Yes. We are home to a once magnificent Tree. Now it is slowly coming to an end; unless, of course, I destroy John the Elder before he gains too much power in his place upon the hill… shall we go?”

The Detective wishes he had not come alone, “Yes, yes of course, you must destroy the Elder to save a tree.”

The man in blue radios for a group of his compatriots to join him. John and Maggie do not know this, but he has used a series of coded letters and numbers to indicate that he is in trouble and that the oncoming units should show extreme caution. He thinks it best to wait for backup before he attempts arrest. He thinks that they will remain in front of him the entirety of the wait.

“Now, Constable, would you please follow me to the back exit, if it exists. We shall give you the grand honor of meeting The Tree. Do not be shocked by the wonders and oddities you may witness here, if your vision be true enough to see.”

“I'll make sure to stay grounded.”

His sarcasm is lost on John and Maggie, now holding hands and looking for the door twelve feet directly in front of them. If the universe had eyes, which we know is impossible, it would see the Detective grow more uncomfortable while watching two people mime at not seeing a door.

“Ah yes! The door appears. Often it is a tricky thing to find exits, don't you concur Maggie?”

“Of course my love. Doors and windows, windows and doors,

can hardly keep a thing straight without a window or a door next to it!"

"Well said! Shall we?" John makes a grand bowing gesture as Maggie walks out. He stays bent over, arms outstretched in supplication to the man in blue to exit.

"After you, Mr. Younger."

"Please, Constable, you must."

"John. Walk out the door. No sudden movements if you please."

John screams, "Of course! Time is an illusion we all attempt to grasp in these dark days. We go on to The Tree!"

In that scream the Detective hears, in horrible clarity, the vibrato of uncertainty. In that scream, he hears John's imbalance. His fractured worldview becomes auditory. To the ears of someone trained to keep balance, to right the world in as binary a way possible, can be heard the tell-tale song of madness.

John screams to Maggie from his mind, or so is his attempt, planning their escape. He knows the Detective is planning to take them in once his compatriots arrive. John tells her to run to the woods. He has provisions hidden in secret paths. They shall run from this office until the police lose interest.

Detective Wilson sees John lean over and stage a whisper to Maggie, "Run to the woods and we will be free.'

"There will be no running," The man in blue speaks as calmly as possible. "Now let's wait here calmly till my friends arrive and we all can have a nice chat."

"Go!"

They run.

He screams for them to stop.

They refuse by increasing pace.

He responds by returning his weapon to its harness and sighing heavily.

"Christ I hate running. Where the hell is my back up?"

# 78. Escape Velocity.

They have slipped into the byways of "The Burned-Over District." Following game trails and hunter's routes they move silently, avoiding Officers who are destined to come.

"John, my darling, where are we heading?" Kali asks to break the silence, already knowing the answer.

"Kali? Where is Maggie? Oh god, we lost Maggie!"

"John, my darling, Maggie is in her place of doors. As she will always be. I will be by your side as I must be. The Child wanders these woods."

"But, wait, she was here, with me. She brought the Detective."

"I know, my darling. It is this way sometimes. Use your sight, and see the reality of us. We are the sword above your head, my sweet. We are Maggie and Kali both. We are Dura and Gideon. We are those that came before, and those which have recently paired. Understand this: there is no separation. We, of the fruited tree, are one person, experiencing itself subjectively. Have no fear for my face is not Maggie's. In the end we all are consumed by this place."

"I feel the truth in your words," John sighs. "We shall move to the place of doors then. Sister Maggie will house us. From there, we will see."

John is pensively clenching and relaxing his fist, a primal heartbeat to stave away reality, or so it would appear to him. The woods echo lightly, their footfalls crunching the autumn fall. On either side of their path, the outline of what was once a rock wall molders barely visible, a forgotten marker of land left to new growth.

They stop to sit upon the ruin of an old farm wall. John moves a large rock from the vanishing wall, and from the hollow beneath pulls out a backpack. From the woods, a series of small footfalls is issued. The outline of The Child moves from wavering existence to something corporeal, into something tangible. John and the girl look upon his arrival in silent nods.

They walk for what seems like hours, until the roof of a Victorian house peaks out from the Trees. As they walk towards that roof, a wall appears, covered in a blanket of moss.

"We have arrived unmolested. Let us call upon this place of doors. Kali I believe it would be proper for you to do the summoning."

Kali, seeing the faint outline of a door in the nearly unbroken moss, pulls off clumps of green, tossing them to the ground.

An oxidized knob is revealed from the vegetation, testament to the outline's original usage.

She grunts with effort as the knob is tested.

The rusting handle and lock give way to her exertions, one last use before obsolescence.

The movement of the door screams out like dying mechanical animals, their death rattle amplified by the cries of dying hinges.

"Well chosen, Kali. It looks as if our entry will be without drama or navigational distress."

"Indeed. The house is welcoming. Let us find its mistress." The Child's utterance startled John, his tongue has been quiet since before they left the Detective in the yard.

"Maggie. It is us, of the office. Are you in?" John calls to the empty space of the house. There is no reply.

"That's strange. It is not often the holder of this place leaves their post. Let us wait in the room of couches for her return."

They navigate the piles of newspapers and sundry filth to find the front room, now clean from Maggie's presence. They see her seated on the couch, staring without sight at the black screen of the television, its antenna dusty and cobwebbed. She is barely visible, as if her body were out of sync with the room, the couch flickering in her faces, transparent masks cycling from familiar to unknown.

"Maggie?" John and Kali ask in unison. She does not reply or seem to hear them. John approaches and sits beside her. Maggie turns slightly in recognition.

"Oh, John of the office! I had not heard you enter. And Kali, The Child, oh the wonders this day brings! Please be at home in this place of doors. Would you like tea or other frivolous things as offering of acceptance?"

"No. We are quite sated. Maggie, we are in trouble. The law of this place has found us guilty of some nonsensical thing. Will you abet us till we figure out what is best to do from here?"

"No. This is a place of law. You will not find shelter here."

"What? Maggie, it's us! You're of our kind, how can you not protect us?"

"I seek to protect only the doors here. That is my charge. John, Kali, Child, you must leave this place."

"Maggie, my darling in mind and soul, how can you do this thing?" Kali asks, heartbroken.

"I can do it because I know my duty, as you all have forgotten yours. John, you know where you should be. And it is not in this place of doors."

"Where would that be?"

“The hill. You belong on the hill. Only then, when you have returned that place to its natural order, will you be welcome again. I wish you luck.”

And with that, her eyes glazed over once more, stuck in perception of something unknown.

“Maggie?” John shakes her shoulder gently. “Can you hear us?”

“She's gone John. A door has been opened, one that only you can close. Let us take our leave from here.” The Child is noticeably annoyed, almost impatient in his speech. “I do not cherish being where I am not wanted. Let the marionette of Maggie remain here, and let us be gone.”

“Yes, in her way she shows us our path. Let us end this farce today. Child, Kali, let us go to the hill. We will end this before the laws of this place call us guilty again and the Elder grows even more so.”

## 79. If there is a real world, this is not it.

I am ready to tell you that there are no police in this town. There is a small precinct for the county, recently defaced in an act of seemingly random violence. The Officer on night watch was knocked unconscious by unknown assailant(s) in a stumblingly daring escape.

This is not true. It never happened.

But, as far as the law is concerned, it is the reason given, and the reason being acted upon. I am ready to tell you that there is a group of uniformed men looking for the workers and residents of a certain house in a certain wood.

It should be known now that the Officers of one town over are driving towards that selfsame house in the woods to attempt an arrest. I am also willing to now go on record to state that the house in the woods is currently being evacuated. The residents are moving into the paths in the woods, slowly driving their way to a certain hill with a certain derelict factory full of dead machines and driving impetus of fractured psyches and memory.

Sirens and lights move under suburban street lamps. Sirens and lights move towards the old logging roads in the woods, the ones wherein sit a few scattered buildings and one remaining old mansion, steadily emptying. Sirens and lights move loudly through streets onto dirt roads, dust flying into the air like flocks of birds streaking the moonlight.

Sirens and lights stop movement near a rotted stump: a rusted car; an artifact from a bygone day; both mechanical and vegetable; both rusted in the rain of years passing.

Blues and guns stride powerfully to the front door screaming things and kicking others.

Guns and blues do not greet an old couch or look for cookies made from local flora.

Blues and guns do not smile whimsically at brass lined computers or false greenhouses in bathrooms.

The guns and the blues are not amused by the kaleidoscopic eye in the brass machine or the wonder of doors in the basement; nor are they happy by the lack of people in the house.

Blues and guns curse loudly, one even goes so far to tip over a perfectly placed chair. The record player looks on in silence.

The blues and their guns move to the back yard, unimpressed by a monstrous tree with wondrous fruits given to man to open the channels of mind left blocked by the society for which they hold their guns for.

They are unimpressed with the rotted car, the empty sheds, and the lonely bicycle.

They signal for their compatriots to join them. They wonder where to find our stalwart heroes. No one, not gun nor blue, takes notice of the path leading into the woods, the one on which adults and The Child theoretically walk towards a mutual end.

## 80. The Magician: Woods, revelations, and the loveliest fruits.

The Child who is a man speaks with grace, with a cadence of authority, of learning. “It's time for a greater quantity of openness in our talks John, the youngest of this grouping.”

“I believe that time is here. This is truth.” Kali echoes.

“What is left to say? How could there still be boxes yet unopened? Please, I think all things should be known by now.”

They are guided by a wooded path.

They are walking on an upward gradient, to the empty place on the hill.

They are moving towards the inevitable end of this narrative variant.

They are, as perceived by John, moving through a testament left on a red notebook.

They are chained in a red notebook slowly filling with blue ink connective tissue.

They stand in convocation under a canopy of trees.

The thing perceived as a child is about to give out something related to wisdom to John. John will internalize it as a form of story, that moves his hero's journey from a failed artist, to Hercules standing triumphant over the remnants of a villain.

We watch as a story unravels from the ink:

"John, as well you know, the Elder awaits you on the hill. Also, as well you know, the Elder is an ephemeral concept left over from a past which was invented by Hephaestus to move you to this point. You must realize that what you seek on the hill could be found in the office, or in the place of doors. With this, you will destroy that part of you which still needs this villain to be destroyed. You will be freed."

"Child. Did you say that Hephaestus invented the past?"

Kali steps in to elaborate and calm the growing discomfort of John, "Yes my love. Hephaestus wrote a story for you. In which you become the hero and leader of this group. He made you in his image. You, as you know, are manager *in nominus*. This is not an idle phrase. He, not unlike the gods of the other place, spoke you into existence."

"So, the past, as I understand it, is untrue? There was no conflict, no tearing of the sky, no Elder John betraying Hephaestus, no periphery invading our space, no truth?"

"Oh John, of course not! And, by that, I mean, of course! Most of the narrative, as perceived by you through the filter of Hephaestus was, and is true, except for the invented parts… the purposeful lies… and the ubiquitously untrustworthy narrator. There is no truth here; however, we have made our best attempt to elaborate something sensible from the tumbling chaos of observation through tools poorly fit for the task."

Kali is calm, but growing frustrated. She had thought that John had understood more of this.

"You don't know the truth, either?" John is lost, again. He is struggling with one of the fundamental concepts of this place. He will learn. Or, he will not, and the hill will swallow him.

"John, I am sorry we were not clearer in the past. I, and my esteemed colleague Kali, had assumed too much about your natural proclivity towards the nature of this place. John, remember, the map is not the territory. The narrative, the story of us, is just that: a story. It is a fiction to describe something far less tangible. Do not believe your narrators, or all you will know is a story. There is no truth to be grasped. The periphery is simply that, the sides of an agreed upon awareness, nothing more solid than a platonic form or the movements within a kaleidoscope."

"So, am I to believe you now, Child and Kali? Should I take your speeches as gospel and doubt my and your past, or is this another fiction?"

They answer in unison: "Exactly."

"Take us as fiction, for we invented all of this for your benefit," Kali is nearly singing.

"Take us for reality, for the nature of reality is manifold," The Child complements in harmony.

They again speak in song: "Do not mistake us for truth tellers. We are simply actors moving within a script."

"I should look between the narrative and the facts. I should see the invented things from the corners of my eyes and take them for gospel. You're right in thinking I had missed an important thing. I had forgotten the nature of the metaphor of the periphery. The animals, the Trees, the ghosts of the other side; they are all placeholders for something unperceived. You are quantum storytellers. By my direct observation, I have changed the story. Jesus. It is so clear. It's a metaphor."

Again, Child and Kali speak in unison: "It is not."

John exhales a gust of disappointment, frustration at his inability to grasp the meaning of their words. He holds his head in his hands and tries to massage the cognitive dissonance from his temples.

"You are right about most, but wrong on that account," the Child continues. "It is not all metaphorical. It is truth, as filtered through metaphor. We use the fruit of our dearest Tree to feed you. It will open the conduits of your mind and let loose the periphery.

We use the fruits to let you perceive the metaphor. There is, in as much as there can be, fact: something on a hill that is built upon our lesser natures; a group of police who think you have murdered and attacked; a gift of sight, which you possess; and a story nearing its end. This is gospel. This is truth."

In this moment, John is as close to understanding as he will be until this thing ends.

"I took communion from The Tree, and so I was open to the periphery. From that point on, I was to see the world as metaphorical as well as factual. I was to see the periphery, and was lost within it. Now I see the angle as just that. Thank you Child, Kali. I know what waits."

Gravity shifts as The Child speaks, "Your demons are waiting to be exorcized John. Let us wait in the office, or the house, or the woods. Let us be your narrative thread in these short hours between your life and its end."

Kali strokes his cheek. "End your demonic ways, John, my darling, and return to the one world of the office. Begin a new life. Bring forth a new generation, born from the blood of your expurgated sins."

"Or fail. And resign yourself to a prison made by yourself, of yourself. We shall have no further input. We return to being simple puppets, dancing on narrative strings pulled by a maniac."

# 81. A policeman, with a penchant for conspiracy theory.

In a small police department in a quiet town, a man wearing predominantly blue is sitting behind a desk. Upon his head, an icepack, upon his desk, reports from the town and handwritten notes on scraps of paper. Across the notes grow a line of theories ranging from the Kennedy Assassination to the cults hiding in the recesses of "The Burned-Over District."

In a small police department in a quiet town evidence of drug use is found in the form of desserts cooked with certain plants. In that same place, the man behind the desk is getting nervous. In that same place, the man behind the desk is wishing they had cameras, so he could have told the truth. He would have to tell his Sergeant of his mishandling of prisoners held for questioning. He would have to explain to the straight laced, straight postured, bastion of lawfulness that he had gotten distracted, and somehow let one John "The Younger" Weishaupt escape from a locked cage in a secure building.

In the universe, a wave of probability is flowing out from the outer rim of a galaxy which once housed a civilization much like ours. That wave will hit soon enough, and the town will move on, unaware. The man in primarily blue behind the desk shivers in a primal notion of that probability wave, and its possible outcome. He wonders how long he has until the others see him differently, a compromised entity thing in the shell of a once proud compatriot in arms. He wonders when they will change from seeing him as a good man to seeing him as a drug made manifest, his life condensed to a vibration soured by the laws of that place. He wonders if he simply caught John again and ignored the incident, could he possibly get away with not telling his commander?

# 82. Collisions.

In a small circle of dirt, The Child, John, and Kali stand, marking points of a rune made by happenstance and fortune.

In the woods, in a small dirt circle, in the closing moments of a generation, three actors take a moment to collect what is left of themselves.

In a wooded area the cycles of the world are again strangely mimicked, as self dissolves in the wake of destiny.

The Child looks into John's eyes. John sees himself reflected therein, a man grown, marching towards entropy. In the eyes of The Child, John sees the way of things, maddening and confused. He sees false hallways and invisible doors. He sees his friends combining and splitting. He sees that Maggie and Kali are spirals within the other. He sees them smash into one another and repel, combine and fall apart. He watches them dance as dipoles of liquid metal, as a feminine energy wave, moving from Maggie to Kali to Dura and back again.

In the spinning gravity well of the office in the woods he sees that pieces of himself are breaking off to become Hephaestus, are falling to the floor to become The Child. Those liquid forms collide and become like his father, exploding back into Tyler, his once broken kin. In a maelstrom of energies the thought forms of the office bounce, melt, collide and coalesce, until a shimmering pool sits static upon the floor. From that static pool, a waterspout of energy springs up, and becomes, once again, John, of various natures. The pervasive illusion of a separate self reasserts itself once again at the forefront of the probability wave that is John the Younger.

And so, with the last of themselves put back together, they continue the walk uphill into the reaches of a finale. John, in the lead, is striding forth as if imbued with a greater awareness than he had previously known, driving forth to find a villain, to find a father, to find himself. He goes forth to find a rusted gate with a hole the size of a child. He moves forth to pass through that energy that had repulsed him earlier. He walks forth to spin the poles of the magnet, and recombine with that other self, split asunder by time and the machinations of guilty thought.

## 83. A final push.

They are compelled through the woods by the fever within John. They are forced forward by his speeding legs, by his keen insight. He knows, after all this time, that this is something that has to be done. He knows that this has already been done, and done again, long before the utterance of his name. The fight in the basement with the phantom thing comes rushing back into John's mind as they move with a hope-tinted anxiety through the silted air of the woods towards an adversary as perceived. Kali holds a small torch, its flame flickering in the gloaming. The child follows with mechanical precision. The beams from The Child's flashlight propel them like the pole of an unseen gondolier.

He thinks, 'Am I ready for this? Can I possibly fix myself and this world? I feel Hephaestus calling from the Trees. I feel myself as a blank slate filling with yet illegible scripts. I feel the weight of some metaphor upon me, not knowing whether to shrug it off or carry it as a token of my trials in this place.'

As they are compelled up the hill, Kali looks to John and sees the image of a young Hephaestus drunk on new power and the fruit of the then flourishing Trees. Her long dress torn near the bottom, muddied with the wear of the day; her hair falling from a forever failing barrette. She feels the pulsing of the night air as the denizens of the periphery scream and lash in the night. She walks up the hill as weeks of symbols and hallucinations run through her memory. She feels herself as if she were three people in one, all speaking as an echo from a similar source.

As they are compelled up the hill.

The Child with the voice of a man sees symbols in the stars

and ghosts in the periphery. His flaxen hair is tangled from exertion and the entropy of a fate made manifest. He feels this chapter moving towards its end. He feels the circle becoming complete, a man laid to rest as another rises, the way of kings and peasants alike, the circle of birth and growth, death and seeding.

The Child follows John dutifully up the hill, watching symbols in the sky, knowing the world will be changed by the morning. The Child follows, knowing that the world will still be the same by the morning.

The Trees shake as if alive, as if they possessed the same animating spirit as the Trees belonging to the periphery. In that motion, shapes are seen moving from branch to branch, wavering in the moonlight. Upon the ground, the hounds of that other place hunt the group from the shadows and from the underbrush. In the house upon a hill the Elder whistles tunelessly, signaling an end.

They attack.

From the air erupts a wave of black wings, tearing apart the still night. They scream down from above in shrill voices, falling in and out of audibility, a pulsing wall of sound and vision beating across the night. The child ducks as Kali pulls him into her arms, cradling him from the attack. John stands, transfixed by the random motions and excitement. His face is turning red with the scrapes and cuts from wings of arguable existence.

From the ground a growl echoes out, and another. A symphony of noise moves towards the crouching shapes of Kali and The Child. John stands transfixed as his jeans begin to tear, slowly staining red from the efforts of these beings.

Kali and The Child hold closely, whispering whatever words of comfort they feel is needed as the blood and noise become too much. They await entry to the other side, accepting that the loss they now face is the last. There are no more barriers to hold back this wave, no more offices in fantasy woods to stop the actions of a teacher gone corrupt. In the woods John stands, eyes open and bloodshot from the assault, staring at a rift in the sky, invisible to the birds and dogs now gnashing at him. In the woods a child and a young woman hold each other as they begin to bleed. On the hill, above the woods, a man pretends he still exists.

In the woods, the trees are soaking in the blood and jetsam brought forth by the denizens of the other side. In the woods the Trees are lifeless, waiting for a spark of imagination and ingenuity to transform them from wood to blood, from vegetable to mystical. In the woods, trees debate their dual nature as a fight to the death is boiling at their bases.

## 84. Once more with feeling: the story of dead men.

Theoretically, once upon a time, a large man and a thin man spoke to one another with the language and tonality of friends.

Once, theoretically, upon that time, they broke ranks over a minor debate about the fate of humanity. One, the thinner, believed a system of forced words and dramatic deeds were the way to mend the fractured universes. Another, the larger, felt that positive and thoughtful words, tinged with whimsy and the sense of something magical, were the way to lead packs to reunion.

One walked up a hill.

One stayed in a sylvan valley.

They spoke but once after the fall. They spoke with joyless voices sapped of inflection, of energy. They spoke of laws and philosophy, of a holographic universe designed by chance and maintained by decay. They spoke.

“It's strange, lying dead above my Tree,” the once booming voice of Hephaestus meekly uttered.

“Yes. Death has a way of defining generations. This narrative seems at stasis.”

“Stasis is a good word. Our narrator must wait for years now.”

“Our narrator will wait. An ad will be placed. A recruit will come and we will move towards the end of a story told to various deaf ears.”

“A blind man wrote us. His work is poor. I will refuse when it is my calling."

"My darling John, I am sorry for your choice. But I was written to bring him up; as we were written to be supplanted. Our names are written as the first. Our names will be the ones to be repeated, as they have before been chanted in the place of the others."

"Indeed, my brother, father, lover and manager ex-nominus. Be at peace until then. The other place will flow into here and you will be forced into battle."

"Indeed. So it is. So it was. Let us play our parts well and let a universe be joined by time or force. Good life John, my dearest."

"Good life Hephaestus, your acting was the best, let our writer be kind in your exit."

## 85. John finally makes up his mind about something.

A swarm of shadow birds, insects, and the ubiquitous shadow-creatures are gnashing, biting, scratching at Kali, Child, and John. Chunks of skin, blood, and hair are falling to the forest floor. Kali throws her torch in a last, useless attempt to protect John and The Child. The child flares his oarsman flashlight, and chants songs from the Trees. John is frozen.

His sight, his grasp of the periphery, fails to push back the menace. His only weapon discovered to be impotent.

He, as when he first arrived, is in an unknowable situation. He, as when he first felt the fear of seeing into the periphery, is left without defense. His only weapon, as perceived, has shown itself as useless.

Then, from the deep reptilian recesses of John's mind, a click is heard. A layer of connective tissue is formed, sinew built up, and the final association, so long dancing at the sides of his awareness, is made.

"It's fake."

He looks to Kali and The Child in their torn and bloodied rags. He looks to the sky, and the trees, to the ground and to the other side.

"I was so wrong. This is the puppet world. This is the simulacra. I am fake. There is no John," he laughs in relief. "How stupid I've been. There is no I. There is no observer. Silly, silly, me."

The shadows and trees stop their manic gyrations. They freeze in defiance of Newton, floating stones demarcating the ideas that were, in that moment, shown to be insufficient.

The shadows and the motions cease.

What is left is a group of three, standing with empty lungs and invisible wounds. John, as perceived by himself, is with his staff, clean and unfractured, standing under trees lit by the diffused light of stars, long since finished.

"Kali, Child, it is over. I understand. The other world, the ruins, the birds, the Trees, the dogs, I get it. Dualities, nothing more complex than dualities, we are the manifestation of a story weighted at the ends. This is narrative. Narrative, and I have decided to rewrite an ending chosen poorly in a hypothetical past. Those things were never here. We are perfect."

"John my darling, you have shown an awareness that only the founders can rival. Bless their names."

"Yes. I am glad to call you manager. You are truly worthy of your honored name. Your forefather would be proud. You are so much like him, before his turn."

"I am nothing like him. Yet, I am him. Hephaestus and my other were sides of a coin. For him to diverge as such was like that coin landing on edge. I shall push forward and let it land."

"Does the plan change? Do we move upon the hill?" Kali shows confusion for the first time in memory.

"We move to the hill. I have something to show you there. I believe I know how to describe the motions and their inherent energies. I know the spot on which this story will find its cessation."

## 86. Arrival.

John is walking, eyes firmly fixed on the gate ahead. Kali and The Child follow him, with sullen steps. He approaches the hole in the gate he entered once as a child, once as a lost young man, and now, as a leader of men… or, at least, a leader of a pretty young lady and a distorted archetype of a child.

"This is it. The end of all things," John speaks with the gravitas of foreknowledge that he will succeed here. He will not be repulsed like the last time he approached. Hephaestus had forgiven him of the sins he committed here. Guiltless, he leads them on.

"I'll hold open the fence, please come through Kali, Child."

They approach a collapsing pile of rusting metal and broken concrete slabs. John's eyes begin to water, catching the attention of his companions.

"Child, Kali, how much did he tell you of my past?"

They answer in unison: "Nothing."

"I assumed as much. He was a man to be trusted." John clears his throat, and pulls down the hem of his shirt. "This pile in front of us is the cause of this story. This pile of metal and dust once held the blood and stilled heart of my brother, Tyler."

John takes a deep breath, trying to keep his eyes and head clear, "I failed him as an older brother, and because of that he died. I was left in ruin, broken… I invented a world where he still lived; where we were still a traditional family, one without ghosts."

John stalls for a moment, collecting his newly crystallized

thoughts. “I was broken, hateful, and worthless. Until I met a girl who let me relax, who thought I was worth something. Until I met Hephaestus who showed me that everything is a product of vision, that we create one another. And now, we stand upon the marker of a horrible day and will push forth upon the past the apologies and awareness of the now. I am the schism in the other world. I am the Elder, and the Fool. I am Hephaestus James Bonobus. Most importantly, I am John the Younger, and I will bring forth balance, since it is my role and duty to do so. Kali, Child, I am sorry for the reality I have forced upon you. I am sorry that my skills of creation were so unsteady. Beginning in the morning, there will be rebirth, if such a thing can exist.”

## 87. A terrible end to a group of wonderful people.

Do you remember that star we spoke of earlier? Well, it was a bit of a planet-centric notion that it did nothing in particular. Unfortunately, that star's light is now hitting a planet. That planet is now irradiated; its atmosphere's inability to block that specific style of photon proving its demise. A collective scream of pure horror and hopelessness could be heard if there were ears to hear; there are none. The dreams, hopes, aspirations of a planet doomed with a momentary, unseen particle. From the periphery, their destiny was written into the ash, ever decaying.

The potentiality of those waves, of that far away scream, no longer propagate, so is stopped the propagation of the story that is currently closing. The words of a generation draw to a close, a reality destroyed in unheard anguish and mute screams moves towards inevitable oblivion. From the periphery of the high castle on the hill, a group of bedraggled survivors approach, momentarily unseen, bringing with them the story of Death, destroyer of worlds.

## 88. Video game logic leads us to an end.

They stand in a triangle in front of the run-down concrete edifice on the hill. From within, the echoing sounds of machines dying reverberate on the chill air. A red and yellow glow is flashing from within, through a layer of implied mist the lights dance in forms of humans and monsters.

The Child speaks softly.

"John, we know what is in there. Do not fear it. Simply see him as you would anything else since your arrival with us. See him for what he is, an extrapolation of the previous generation, a relic holding on for too long. Do not fear it and you will be purified. The office will be allowed to be re-staffed, the Trees allowed to once again flourish."

Kali holds John's hand, lightly.

"My darling, please, do as instructed. It is in the performance of ritual that our insights come. Let us dance one more time as servants of the Elders, then be done with their generation. This night will mark the birth of a new order of the followers of the peripheral. Let us have it be done right."

Kali kisses John lightly upon the lips, smirking. John stands bemused yet strengthened by the belief of his compatriots. Wordlessly, he turns from their triangle and approaches the door. It shimmers in implied light, the dust and mist of the other side dancing off the lights from the decaying interior. The force he felt on the first visit returns to him, pushing him back. He tries, red-faced in struggle, to push his way through the barrier, to enter the place upon the hill. His eyes slam shut as he leans forward against the invisible wall, pressing forward, until exhaustion sets in. He falls to the dirt, staring into the inaccessible finish. Kali and Child join him.

"I…." he stammers, "I failed."

"No, John. You have not yet succeeded. We will figure a way in." Kali holds his hand, still hot from the exertion.

"John. Did not Hephaestus, our previous master, give you means of access upon his demise?"

"No. He did not. All I received was the book and the… oh… the key. How could I have forgotten! Our Hephaestus did have a flair for the dramatic. But, there is no lock."

The Child speaks with authority. "John, you must challenge that statement with grander visions. Create the lock and use the key. Bind this world to the other and let us cross over into this unwelcoming place."

Taking the key from his bag, John feels its weight in his hand. He walks to the doorframe still crackling with residual energy from his recent attempt to enter and concentrates his sight, aligning his body with his awareness.

He enters.

There is no force pushing him back, no squirming animals or shadows in the corners. He stands in a dusty room, dilapidated, full of dead machines and illegible graffiti. To his left sits a rusted lump of copper, a remnant of velvet hanging from its top. To his right a door marked 'W.C'. In front of him another door, marked with flourishing inlays of engraved flowers and roaming lines. He turns his head to Kali and The Child, motioning them to follow. They approach cautiously.

"It is a mimic of the office, dead," The Child's voice holds a tremolo unfamiliar to John.

"It is a dead office, Child," Kali's voice trembles. "The Tree was uprooted. The work became false. This is a failed mimicry of our place. A one-act play canceled on the first night. It is an insult."

Kali spits upon the floor, cursing under her breath, "The sooner we end this, the sooner we can replant and rebuild. This place will house the visions of a new Tree soon enough."

They walk carefully through the industrial detritus, stepping lithely over metal bramble and paper boulders. The Child points at a door at the back of the room, barely discernible from the rest of the wall. They proceed towards the phantom door as the sounds of metal on metal fill the air.

"The Elder. I can see the patterns dispersing. This place is chaotic energy. I can feel his presence," John senses his namesake. He shivers in recognition of the all too familiar energy. "I'm in there. His energy is like mine. I know this man."

# 89. Alternates.

The Child, as perceived by the universe one over, would be, at this very moment, hearing the sounds of police shovels digging up the grave to this right. An old house with odd doors as backdrop.

In the grave next to The Child, in front of a house with too many doors, the body of a once beautiful woman lays motionless.

Or so the constabulary would lead us to believe. Or so the universe next door would lead us to think.

The alternate view is that a shift has occurred, from the weighted left foot of the past to the swinging right leg of the future. The usefulness of old names are coming to a close. The burials of old clothing and outdated furniture in the holes left by uprooted bulbs, are the sole reminders of an old man obsessed with the doors and trinkets of a group he left behind.

The whispers of police, and the rumors of the town conflate. The voice of someone perceived gone still speaks in the other place.

Cassiel, as perceived, if one can perceive these things, is walking down a one-way street in a quaint town.

He smells smoke and hears sirens. The hill in the distance is yellow and orange.

He whistles tunelessly. He fingers a small, plastic dinosaur in his coat pocket.

His breath shows upon the night as he exhales the lyric-less melodies of an enterprise left to wanton ruin, a favor for an old friend. A bottle of brandy is in his backpack, a snifter carefully wrapped in newsprint.

He fingers his plastic talisman as he walks his old routes, tracing runes in a map as accurate as could be made without the advantage of a view from above.

He walks in purposeful circles towards a dilapidated police station and courthouse.

He wonders when the funds to regain his place in the community will come, his sundries once again left out to be unsold.

He walks with a bag of gifts.

He walks towards a celebration of an action yet unaccomplished, brandy and snifters at the ready.

## 90. The Fool(spinning).

The office on the hill sits silent.

A whiff of smoke in a black room, and a scurry of animals are the only signs of life. John the Younger, The Child with a Man's Voice, and Kali of the Desk step lightly towards the inner reaches of the office.

From a far off place they can hear the sounds of conflagration, the smoke growing stronger.

From that far off place they can hear a familiar voice whispering.

From that far off place, John the Elder walks circles in a useless room, a fire burning at its center.

They walk slowly, not to be heard, towards the smell of smoke and the now visible orange of flame. A shadow walks across the room, and there's a sound of a door closing. They follow into a room, now half gone with flame. They step quickly through the room, almost unlivable from the heat. They find a pair of doors, one left, one right.

"Kali, Child, what do we do? To use the same door would send us to different places. I do not wish to separate." John's concern is palpable.

"My dearest John! How lovely you are even in this time of flame and revenge. You shall take the left and us the right. I give you my word that we shall be reunited."

Kali holds The Child's hand as they approach the doors. John, taking from his pack the small ax given to him by the phantasm Hephaestus approaches the left-most door. Kali, with a purposefully deep breath, approaches the right most.

John sees, for the first time, fear in the eyes of The Child. John had thought of him as some kind of preternatural prophet; the emotions of a child unsuited to his grace. "Be wary. Be calm my boy."

John pats him lightly upon his tiny back while making the briefest of contact with Kali's eyes. The Child looks up to them both, a false family joined in the ritual of seeing the periphery. They break their triangle covenant as Kali and The Child walk through the door on the right, finding themselves in a copse of trees.

Nearly blind from the night they can make out an orange glow further into the woods. The Child looks up to Kali, and she looks to him. They grasp hands and move towards the orange glow. The Trees watch on with disinterest. They walk in dark woods towards an orange light. If they had eyes better suited for the dark, they would see a familiar tree, moving against the wind, its fruit jutting out as grotesques on the natural cathedrals of the woods. If they had eyes to see, they would see the flowering of the new generation; it's nature to be decided by a conflict shaping on a hill near a now flaming building.

John opens the door on the left, listening to the sounds of Kali and The Child moving through the right. He closes his eyes and steps forward through the doorway. Looking around him, he sees the office on the hill, the grass of the field firmly under foot, Kali and Child nowhere in sight.

A shadow is pacing back and forth upon the grass, hissing and spitting out words of venom and spite. The shadow points and gestures with grand, meaningless motions. It flails and spins, falls and rises, like some puppet Gurdjieff manipulated from the branches of unseen trees.

It stops to look upon John the Younger, its vision burning in the cool autumnal air. The Elder's blackened face twists into a rictus, welcoming his other self back upon the hill with a flourished bow.

He speaks.

"My son! Welcome and know that you have lost. He is dead and I have found a home here upon this hill. Work with me, my bastard son, and we shall shape the names of the ones to follow. We will be Hephaestus again, but vastly improved by harsh lessons of time. You will again realize that we are one in the same. We are the same matter experiencing itself subjectively. I do not exist, John. I am you. Accept that simple fact and we will walk together in that other place. We will make our wills manifest here, and watch the mirrored worlds shape in our wake. The visions of the past will be erased and we, as the rejoined whole, will speak forth a new reality, a new perception. We will be glorious gods of the new world! We will soak in their adulation as the Trees soak in our husks when we are gone!"

"You believe that I am you. I know that you are me. But this entire story is subjective. I see this universe. I allow it to wash over me, making small changes when the time is proper. This universe will grind me to dust when it is proper. You have held our name for too long. You defy the will of decay by holding on to this petty flesh. You use my face and my past to pervert the efforts in the woods, to perfect a methodology of perception. You greedily take from the new ones in gross mimicry of the elder ones. You take from us, the new generation, to keep your failed ideas in play. The rot you bring is an insult to the work of Hephaestus, once your friend and colleague. You insult me, your child and your doppelganger, your father and your other. You insult the woods and the memories held in the ruins of the other place. You, John the Elder, are an insult. Let this be the last time you are named with the language of the woods."

"An insult? No, quite the contrary my boy. I am a compliment to this story. I hold sacred names. I use the language and perceptions of the woods, and of the hill as I see fit. What I am is your peripheral awareness made solid. I cannot be removed from you as long as you can see in the ways of myself and the other elders. What you fail to see is that I will be the nemesis on the hill until such time that I decide to take from you the woods. You are a placeholder for my movements, John, no more, no less."

"Then I will force you back into that other place. I will move you, bodily, into the periphery. I will let the seedlings and their shapeless masters deal with your savagery."

"A fine thought, my child! But you fed too many, too often. The trees are rotting, the fruit moldered. You do not have ability to force me back to the other place. No one but Bonobus could do that, and he is too far gone now, too much a part of the other place to have influence here. John the Younger, I wish for you to come to the hill, and we will be as a pair, just as it once was in the woods and in the darker days before the sky was broken."

"No. I shall remain in the woods. And you will be ended. Hephaestus died to bring me back from a dark place. Now, you will be done. As he has taught me a better way to live, so shall I teach you a better way to be reborn. Let it be done, Elder. Let us walk you back to that other place and you can be, again, part of this glorious cycle. First you must be broken down, and then the Trees will feed from you. Then the fruit will spring forth, and that will be yours, and all of our immortality. Come with me and let us visit the ruins."

"John, the lesser. You have no way to take from me my sight. With Bonobus went the chance for your vision's fulfillment. You do not possess the clarity of sight to stop me. I will take from you that Tree and you will rot. Thus, I have written. Your death will mark this place as complete. So our brother died upon this soil, so shall you. Your blood will soak my hill. Your Tree will feed my followers. Your life is forfeit, you do not..."

And so the small ax, a token from the other place, from the other father, shines in a blurring motion through the gloaming.

The sound of wet wood being split echoes across the hill and the valley.

Upon the grass, upon the hill, there is a slumping motion, and a fall into the oncoming dark.

A shadow loses its body.

An awareness is shut off with a simple stroke.

And so it is, that the man's head is split across the brow, spilled upon the world. So it plays, as it has before, his name seeping from the world in a darkening circle around an ax-handle and a stilled form.

From his mouth a stream of red and black, of blood and bile.

From his mouth, rivulets of filth bleed forth into the soil, darkening the grass, soaking into the soil.

From the woods, the forms of a woman and a child appear as darker patches against the growing conflagration, the light of the fire allowing them a clear view. The office on the hill is engulfed, the cinders and ash beginning to fall as snow upon the characters moving through the end of another act.

The eyes of the universe see John staring down at the bloody flow from a stilled body. The eyes of the universe have no influence as he feels revulsion and relief. His own body lies at his feet. His head cleaved in two.

John smiles maniacally at his form, as the ghostly arms of Kali wrap around him. In John's mind the child is giddy, and pacing the lawn, his face reflecting orange from the house.

In John's visions, they sit together, silenced in an act so simple, so unexpected.

From the woods the disturbances of simultaneous movements are heard in an organized rustle.

They speak in the same voice:

"The Seedlings have come."

The small dolls appear from all sides, their wooden eyes unfocused, their mechanical movements painful, yet smooth. They walk with purpose to the dead thing at stage center. They approach, singing in wooden honorifics the now dislodged name:

"We feed John the Elder, so his name may rise again. All bow to John the Redeemer."

They bow with clockwork motion as they each grab at the bloodied body laying prone before them. One for each limb, one for the split head, and with graceful strength they pull him asunder.

The body of John the Elder, of John the Villain, of John the dark aspect of the periphery, by effort and force, is torn into quarters. His head sits, noiselessly propped up by the handle of a small ax.

The limbs carried forth on the wooden backs of the strange creatures from that other place.

The torso, gruesome and naked of extremities, is hoisted by the remaining wooden marionettes.

John smiles broadly, laughing to himself.

They sing to the heads of the gathered members of a phantasmagorical office.

They sing their thanks, internal, as they, skipping, drag limbs and viscera into the woods, onto the paths back to the other place.

The blood soaks the grass on the hill, and John stands.

The ground cries out to the Trees in the valley.

The hill reclaims, the land shutters, as the weight is released.

John is now the owner of this death, the maker of the new house.

John, as he sees the blood pool that was himself, realizes the truth in the words of Hephaestus.

He is dead, as a physical past. What was "he" is nothing but a symbol for a decaying generation moving with increasing entropy.

An awareness of entropy, a vision of what came before, is enough to let John heal.

John of the dead brother; John of the murderous fantasies; John of the detached sense of self, is dead, stilled on a hill in the coolness of spring.

John of the periphery stands tall, cured of the ills of the past. His fear and anger stilled. His name written upon the earth in the imagined blood of a martyr gone these long years. As he put his father to earth, so went his brother. As the past swallowed Gideon, Dura, and Hephaestus, so the present allows John, The Child, Kali, and Maggie to exist as separate entities. As he placed faith in the periphery, they exist until such time that The Tree needs new blood, and another ad is placed.

And John, as a fat old man, will walk himself through a building, on a hill or in the forest; and he will throw whimsy at some splintered person with gifts yet untapped. He will sense the rift and give him books and keys. He will die along with Kali, or Maggie, or child; drifting to that other place as the office is filled with different music, with different voices all calling out from the same place, all calling out with similar songs and names echoing from the past as perceived by an office in the woods. They will dance and feed The Tree. They will eat from The Tree and let themselves be cured. And the circles of what came before will break and reform.

The other place will sit as statuary until it is joined with more of themselves.

With each generation the rubble will clear.

With each generation the rift will suture.

In the night John stands, holding an invisible hand. He poses himself so to look the part of a master orator. He speaks in his deepest tone:

"The Trees will grow in my old blood. The Trees will again mark rebirth. As the ashes fall from the glowing skeleton on the hill, this place will grow again. And I will nourish The Tree, which will mark your return, oh father Hephaestus. We shall feed the Trees and wait upon your return."

The eyes of the universe, if the universe could have them without influence, would see a man standing upon a hill; two others upon the ground. The eyes of the universe, if not for causing an effect on the scene, would see no stilled bodies slowly growing cold. But, the universe will not have eyes, for eyes would cause this scene to unravel, this story to be told as only from one perception, the cat dies as the poison is timed.

The eyes of the universe do not blindly weep as bodies leech their heat into the ground.

The eyes of the universe stare without knowledge, without perception, at the various scenes being played out on the various hills in the myriad perceptions from the multiple players at work.

So the cinders fall from the air, as he stands and watches the last fading embers on the ground in the gathering dawn. Sirens can be heard faintly in the distance. The roots glow again.

So, in the periphery, there is the promise of complete light for those who choose to see. The ground grows cold in the gathering dark. John, the Younger, walks back into the woods with his ghost Kali, hand in hand, singing a wordless song. The Child draws runes upon the sky. All is well in the lands that we choose to look upon.

## 91. The Emperor, the Empress, and the tying up of loose ends.

The dream of an office in the woods filled with odd people and strange philosophy is realized, again. It has been months since the fire, the green shoots of new growth rising from the ashes of the hill. The world has turned right side up again. The world, to that small place, is pure and full of possibility. The ruins of the other place sit in their eternal vigil. The marble shards forever dedicated to the idea that something was better before, and will be again, if the observations are soft, the seers unmotivated and without desire for result.

John, now happily running this little world, bounces and wanders through the office and the woods, playing a game of offices and philosophy. Unburdened of his brother, his father, and his sense that something within him would be shown as broken, or missing, upon observation.

Kali, happily back to her desk in the front office, is typing, blissfully unaware of the parts her ghost self had played in the previous months. The Child in the Yard grows in spurts and tends his tree, healthy and vibrant in the blissful spring. The memories of Hephaestus dance about the place to the rhythm of vinyl played on an old Victrola.

And Maggie, sweet Maggie is currently at the front door.

The ancient bell rings. The man in his late twenties grins and looks up from his desk. The Child tends The Tree. Kali hums to herself. The door opens.

"Maggie," John speaks with a joyous tone. He had seen this

reunion coming in the flickering of his visions, knowing her part in this dream is not yet complete.

Maggie glows at the sight of him. She hold out her open hand, balancing a small, plastic dinosaur.

"A gift."

"My dearest Maggie! How wonderful! A small orange friend!"

"John. I've been thinking about you. Is it okay if I come in?"

"Of course! Maggie, you are always welcome in this place. Care to sit upon the sacred couch?"

"I thought that wasn't allowed?"

"I got a promotion… of sorts. New management, new rules. No use letting a good couch go to waste just because Hephaestus is dead. We all go to The Tree in time, might as well be comfortable in the interim."

"Well, thanks. So, he is dead? The message was a little unclear when we spoke."

"Ah, yes. Learning pains of the place, things are often violently confusing during the curve from observation to awareness… Hah! I sound like him," John smiles wryly. "What I mean is, last we spoke as John and Maggie, I was a little jumbled."

"Oh, jumbled, yes that's about right. I am sorry for his loss. He was a charismatic man. Wish I had more time to know him."

"Yes, well, things tend to circle, from what I've seen. Might be that you and he will sit again in comfortable climes once again," his face is beaming with the vibrations of that place in the woods. Shining with that singular glow shared by those few who can know, but not claim, understanding. "You would enjoy his dances. They were rather, unique."

"My, you seem more chipper than last I saw you. I am happy

things seem to be working out here. Honestly, I was afraid you'd done something dramatic. That night you tried to get me to go to that abandoned house… well, let's just say I wasn't exactly confident that I'd willingly see you again. When I heard that the police were after you… I had pause for concern."

"Hah! Yes, the workings of the mind in this place are often scattered and confused. I am sorry for the scare Maggie. But I can assure you I put those paranoid visions to bed. It's amazing what a metaphorical ax to an invisible head can do to a man in distress."

Maggie looks at him quizzically, "I'm afraid to ask. Metaphorical ax to the head?"

"Yes, that… it is a long story, one for another day. Let us just say the fruit of The Tree causes you to see what needed to be seen in order to be cured; in fact, you would be happy to know I gave 'you' a job and you later stopped talking to us."

"What? I worked for you then didn't talk? How did that happen? Jesus, that Tree must be potent."

"That it is. So much so, that one Constable Seidel was shown to have been under its influence during 'my' daring escape. Thankfully, with Cassiel's return, paired with the fact that Sergeant Smythe was previously employed by Mr. HJ Bonobus, those little law matters were put to an early bed."

"Great! I knew working for a secretive cult in the woods had some perks," Maggie's face becomes slightly flush in the reliving of the light and odd conversations of their first courting. "Did you have to use a secret handshake on the Sergeant?"

"Yes, perks indeed. Also traps, and stillness. But, now, we are all wholly aware and full of memories. Alas, there are no secret handshakes here, though I will take it under immediate advisement. Maggie, I am glad you came back here to see us. The Child and Kali are bound to be excited by meeting you in better circumstances."

"Yes. I would like to talk to them again. I'm still not sure why a child lives in your office with your secretary."

"The path of the periphery is often confusing. But I can assure you that the work done here is both good and lawful. Ask Constable Seidel or Detective Wilson if you need proof. I would be remiss if I did not point out that they, red-faced with shame, visited us here in the woods. The apology was both heart-felt and obviously false. I enjoyed the duality."

"Good. I saw Cassiel. He said that you offered him a job. That's great!"

"Mr. Landry unfortunately declined the offer. He knew Hephaestus, long ago. His part of this play was finished when he pointed me towards this place. He's going to again attempt the opening of the sundries shop. This time with coffee, various biscuits, and some other items people aside from me would actually want to purchase. The work should be good."

"Yeah, I look forward to taking up a seat for hours on end. Now, to the business at hand."

She stands, taking John by the hand, leading him up. Maggie slips out of her shoes and walks him to the bathroom. Wiggling her toes, she looks into his eyes, plaintive and loving.

"I'm ready for my tour now."

John, elated, begins to slip off his shoes, red-faced with effort the second sneaker falls to the floor.

"This way, my dearest. And please continue to hold my hand, for fear we won't meet up again on the other side of the door."

They, hand in hand, enter a door with a sign above it initialed 'W.C.'. The water parts with each step and Maggie's face turns from hesitation to bemusement. In her eyes a wonderland of lush plants and glowing light. She looks to John, and as they share a broad grin, he points to the fish in the floor. From the corner of her eye she spots movement, a subtle shift of light in the shape of a man. Noticing her glance he speaks with the authority of his position.

“Welcome to the periphery, Maggie of the shared glance.”

“I can’t believe my eyes. It’s stunning.”

“Can't believe your eyes… my, what a fine statement!”

The echoes of Hephaestus are again ringing through the halls of the office in the woods. In that tiniest of moments, in that mimicry of one since gone, the cycle is again complete. In the woods of a district now twice burned, the green shoots push forth from ashen soil. In the periphery, a subtle glance has turned to holy writ.

# ABOUT THE AUTHOR

Alexx was raised on the hardscrabble streets of suburban New Jersey. After a stint as a phrenologist[1], he earned a degree in something slightly more useful: Poetry.

Years of wandering the desert with a group of nomadic Bedouin poets[2] lead him to the Pacific Northwest. He currently uses words in Portland, Ore.

Some of his previous work can be found in the collection "the void sutras"

Information on this and other projects can be found at:

http://www.alexxcast.com

[1] This is not true.
[2] Also, completely false.

23934489R00161

Made in the USA
Lexington, KY
28 June 2013